Tales from a Resource Room

The Test

Deborah M. Menenberg

JAT Trax Studios

Uniquely Us – Tales from a Resource Room

www.deborahmenenberg.com

Edited by Linda Franklin
Cover Art by DLR Cover Designs
www.dlrcoverdesigns.com

Publisher: JAT Trax Studios www.jattrax.com
PO Box 230151, Tigard, OR 97281-0151

ISBN-13: 978-1-7362318-2-1
eISBN-13: 978-1-7362318-3-8

This book is dedicated to
My Students

AND

IN MEMORY OF
Jan Marie Trulsen Cook
Who started it all

AUTHOR'S NOTES

We have to laugh together to make it through all the ups and downs. And that is perfectly OK. Special Education is no longer hidden away, or it shouldn't be. However, it once was and, so were the children who were eligible for services. I remember those days, but I can also recall the changes over the last few decades to provide an appropriate and inclusive education for all.

For thirty-six years, I was a Resource teacher. I received a master's degree in Special Education at the University of Oregon in the mid-1970s, around the time Congress enacted Public Law 94-142, The Education for all Handicapped Children Act. Immediately after graduating, I started a Resource Room for students with mild to moderate learning and/or behavior disabilities.

The Resource Room has different names in different schools. And the teacher comes with various titles, but the positions are virtually the same. When I taught in another district, I was the Learning Support teacher, and my classroom was called the Learning Support Room. Regardless of the terminology, this type of classroom is under the Special Education umbrella. The way I see it, once a Resource Room, always a Resource Room.

This book has taken shape in many odd ways and took a ridiculous number of years to write. Every year that I taught, I would keep an envelope in my desk drawer with the words "Funny times of the year." I would collect humorous anecdotes. Early in my career, I took out Envelope One and read it to the staff. Not many were amused. Year after year,

I still compiled notes, but didn't share them until I retired. When I read some to the assortment of guests at my retirement party, everyone laughed. I am not sure if time made a difference, or my odd wit. But what I do know is that in order to survive and meet the daily challenges of teaching, one must realize that it is not the seriousness of the job that is important but the joy of making it successful. I worked with a staff assistant that I used as my inspiration for Mrs. Duchamp in this book. She once told me that we need to always remember the times that drove us to the edge, the times when we laughed together, and some of the things we did to survive.

When my stress or anxiety hit a high note, I would write. This always seemed odd to me as I didn't think of myself as a writer. I would send emails to friends and family. Sometimes I wrote little stories and even plays about the day. In the mid-1990s, a new standardized test, the Washington Assessment of Student Learning (WASL), was expected to be given to all fourth, seventh, and tenth graders in Washington state, where I taught at the time. The testees included those in Special Education as well. Very few were exempt. I thought the world had gone completely crazy.

After that first incredibly difficult year of the WASL, I wrote a little story based on our experiences administering what I considered a ridiculous measure of student achievement. The story was titled "*The Test*," and I gave it to my principal and a few teachers to read. I don't think they were amused. So, it went into the circular file – I thought.

A few years ago, my sister sent me a huge box of "Debbie stories." "*The Test*" was in there as well as a number of other funny tidbits. I started to share them with others and was convinced to publish my stories. *Uniquely Us – Tales from a Resource Room* is intended to be a three-part set: *The Test*, *The Science Fair Project*, and *The Conference*.

Please understand that this particular book is a work of fiction. I do tend to exaggerate, or so I am told. However, the majority of the one-liners and dialogue from the students is correct and contains actual statements. Those bits came from my collective notes in the yearly envelopes. Many of the situations you will read about also occurred, but over time. I mashed together experiences and character personalities and placed them within a one-day time frame. The principal, custodian, and some other adult characters are entirely fictional, but the students are not. I changed their names, but their unique personalities are as real as I remember them.

It is not easy to stay in Special Education for one's entire career. But for me it was the right thing to do. Instead of giving up, I would shake my head and laugh.

CHAPTER 1

The Old West Never Looked Like This

The breath I had been unwittingly holding escaped with an audible groan. Moments after racing from the parking lot through a downpour, I reached the school's side door. I grabbed the handle and tried with all my might to pull it open, but it was locked. Droplets of rain cascaded down my jacket and into my purse as I fumbled inside it to find my keys. Various purse items tumbled out, but I finally managed to grab the keys and then retrieve the bits and pieces that had fallen into the mud puddle beneath my feet. When Rob Holden abruptly marched up beside me, I almost jumped out of my skin while barely managing to stay upright, preventing a full-scale slip into the ankle-deep lake.

"I got this," Rob said, smirking at me. "This door is not typically locked."

"Probably this ridiculous testing protocol," I said, going through my damp possessions. "You are so lucky just being a music teacher."

"Just?" Rob grimaced. "I thought you liked music teachers?"

Rob's smile was bright with an invisible twinkle that I always enjoyed. He was my all-time favorite teacher and best friend at our elementary school. We chatted, laughed, and commiserated daily.

I looked up at Rob and sighed, “I’m sorry. I only meant that at least you don’t have to give this unnecessary, insane standardized test.”

“I am getting strong vibrations that you don’t like testing.”

“Well, they are not good vibrations, I can tell you that,” I added, grunting as I retrieved a few more items and stuffed the wet tidbits back into my purse. “So here it is. Look at this. I finally found the coupon for lunch at the new fast-food place.”

“See, maybe events today won’t be in vain after all.”

“Oh, it’s expired,” I said, stuffing it back into my purse.

Rob unlocked the door, and we entered the chilly hallway. “Got to run,” he said. “Trying to get fourth graders to sing gleefully after testing is a wholly different kind of challenge.”

“Let’s trade jobs,” I shouted to Rob as he raced down the hallway.

I stood in front of my classroom doorway on that waterlogged spring day in 1997. To the left of me on the wall was a printed sign behind a clear plastic covering that simply said, The Resource Room, Mrs. Wright – Teacher. I looked at it and huffed before entering my room.

As I walked in that particular morning, I noticed first the odd stillness. Silence can be refreshing, or it can cause trepidation. I dropped my purse on the corner desk and pulled off my raincoat. Water droplets slid down and danced on the floor as I hung the jacket up on the coatrack. I wondered not for the first time why today would have to be so much different from my typical teaching days. The Resource Room was supposed to be dedicated only to those identified with specific learning disabilities. Every day my students from kindergarten to sixth grade were pulled out of their general education classrooms to receive specially designed instruction for their academic needs. This typically happened in small group sessions. But not today.

My classroom had always been unique in many ways. Although I was frustrated with the upcoming twist on my daily routine, it did make me smile to see this year's theme of the Old West. I looked around as if I was seeing it for the first time. Every year, the Resource Room environment was transformed into a stage set, always something new and fun. My family would surprise me with wonderful ideas and support. Together we created an atmosphere to inspire motivation and fun. I liked to believe that if I felt comfortable and enjoyed the area I had to work in, then so would my students.

I am still not sure if the Old West theme was my sister's idea or mine. Or maybe it was from the rambling thoughts of my students, but somehow it was working. In the far corner where the reading center was located stood a makeshift covered wagon constructed of cardboard and white sheets. The children loved to crawl into it. Not far away was the town mercantile, where we set up a class store with fake money as well as various math items and games. The walls were decorated with amateur drawings of Old West buildings and other historical features. I did put my foot down on the use of guns, outlaws, a saloon, a jail, or even a suggested horse out in the back shed behind the covered play area. It seemed as though students and even some adults whined about the lack of authenticity daily. I often told pretty much anyone who would listen that it was an impression of an Old West town, not the real McCoy.

"What do you think?" a voice asked, shattering my quiet musings.

My eyes quickly darted around the Old West before I ventured a guess. The thin, long stretch of my closed lips was automatic. How was I supposed to answer such a confusing, nebulous question? Or was it supposed to be rhetorical?

"Well?" Mrs. Duchamp, my assistant, asked again, but this time I realized she truly did want a real and honest answer. During the early days of my teaching career, Mrs. Duchamp would have been called my aide, and later a Resource Room assistant. This terminology had also evolved over the years. I think by 1997 the politically correct expression was "paraprofessional." I never liked that. Para does not seem fitting. Why couldn't we just keep the title "aide"? If it was good enough for the state department, it should have been good enough for us. Mrs. Duchamp told me once that when the kids just called her Mrs. D, all was right in the Resource world.

I shrugged my shoulders and sighed. "I don't think our Special Education students should have to take this outrageous standardized test. Why doesn't anyone at the educational top understand that our kids have already been tested to the gills? Just to be diagnosed with a learning or behavioral disorder takes a mountain of assessments, not to mention what must occur before they even become one of our Resource students. Have I mentioned being buried in paperwork?" I was on a roll before I noticed Mrs. Duchamp's crinkled forehead, misty eyes, and solemn expression.

"Oh," she lamented.

"Don't mind me. I am a little wound up," I said with a long-drawn-out sigh. I doubted she was even remotely convinced.

"Yes, I know," she added while walking over to the coatrack with a bundle of paper towels.

My eyes quickly darted around the room, desperately searching the source of her visual discomfort. I focused on the refreshment tables full of snacks provided by the parents, PTA, and the school. "Of course, there it is," I said with a hopeful smile.

Mrs. Duchamp shook her head and finally laughed. "Let me suggest you turn your attention toward our new calendar by the Old West post office bulletin board. I finished it this morning while you were at another one of those meetings at the district office you often complain about, I mean, discuss almost calmly with me. Look, I put a cowboy hat on today's date, April 1."

"So, this testing and all that food is an April Fool's prank. Great! I get it!"

"Well, maybe the food, but don't celebrate just yet. I hear our little darlings stampeding down the hallway."

"What is all that racket? The only students that should be walking down here right now are our six fourth graders," I replied.

In a split second, Mrs. Duchamp and I looked at each other as we raced toward the open doorway. The hallway of our elementary school was wide. The walls had beautifully framed professional artwork interspersed with posters, school projects, bulletins, and an assortment of student assignments. I always thought it was odd the district would spend money on artwork when we had six hundred students and numerous staff that could easily cover the walls with a varied assortment of childhood memories. Yet who was I to run afoul of administrative mandates? I was only a Special Education teacher. Or, as I previously mentioned, my actual title was Resource Teacher, as it says on the sign by the doorway.

As Resource Teacher, I evaluated, diagnosed, developed individualized education plans (IEPs), and taught children with learning and/or behavioral disabilities. My students would be considered mild or moderately handicapped. These children were students who typically had failed in the general education classroom and curriculum without necessary support and assistance. General education teachers knew when they had a student who lagged behind the others in one or more subjects. When this happened, the child might be referred for Special Education services. Sometimes the discrepancy between academic achievement and potential was obvious but only slightly significant. Other times it could be devastating to the educators, family, and the child. These students were often smarter than anyone gave them credit for. They typically had a surprising way of looking at the world and adjusting to the environment around them. Social interactions could be bewildering at times. But these were my kids and I adored them – usually.

CHAPTER 2

What's the Rush – Whoever You Are

"Slow down, slow down. What's the rush?"

"There you are, Mrs. Wright," Sam shouted as he pushed past the others and skidded into the room. "My real teacher said we had to hurry down here before you escaped."

Katie stopped abruptly right in front of me with barely two inches to spare. Either because she was tall or I was short, Katie's head reached right under my chin. She glared up at me, breathing deeply, crossed her arms, and in dramatic fashion announced that the boys were not following the rules. "I hope you will do something about it this time, Mrs. Wright, because these boys are out of control yet again!"

"Thank you for your continued support, Katie. I'll get right on it," I replied, a sweet smile pasted on my face.

I held out my arm to lean against the door frame. Katie was the first to pop under it and head straight to the snack bar. Mrs. Duchamp was on her heels in a flash.

"Whoa, everyone. Slow down. Wait, wait. Hang on. Unless I forgot how to count, there are too many of you," I said.

Tom looked me straight in the eye, "My guess is that you forgot how to count. I did happen to mention that very fact to my dad when he tried to do my homework last night."

"No, she did not forget how to count!" Katie yelled back. "There are extras here, Mrs. Wright. Their teachers said you could use a few more kids and they needed quiet or peace or something like that."

A short, stocky boy with a curly mop of unruly red hair and large round spectacles came lagging behind the others. "My name is Laine, but everyone calls me Lame for reasons I can't fully comprehend."

"I know the reason," Katie said to no one in particular.

Jimmy quickly jumped around Laine. "I think he is in my class, Mrs. Wright." Jimmy had been one of my students since kindergarten. He was full of life. I had often said that I wished I had an ounce of his energy. Beanpole thin, he wore the same baggy clothes every day. His mother told me that the only way she could get him to change is if he totally could not fit into them any longer. That would be soon as Jimmy was growing like a weed.

Laine pushed back around Jimmy as he spoke directly to me. "If Jimmy gets to come here, then I should, too. He is always returning to class and telling everyone how cool it is. Mrs. Wells gets pretty hot under the collar. I know Jimmy doesn't know very much, so how does it work? If I flunk a spelling test, can I come here, too?"

I could only shake my head slightly and whisper to Laine, "Go ahead and come in for today. I will talk to Mrs. Wells later."

"Did you hear that, Jimmy?" Laine said. "I get to be like you."

Good heavens, I thought to myself as I took a step into the hall and addressed each child. “OK, let’s see who is here. Sam and Katie are in the room already.”

“Figures,” Tom said.

“Tom, you are welcome to go in and sit down at your desk.”

“Why? My desk isn’t where it should be,” he said as he craned his head around to look inside the doorway.

“You don’t need to stay out here. Go in and find a seat.”

“Why? I kind of like it in the hall. There’s more action out here.”

“Not for long, so go in,” I said, ignoring him and returning my gaze to the others. “Jimmy and Laine, you can go in, too, and find a desk. And do not push them together. They are exactly six feet apart due to testing regulations.”

“Mrs. Wright?”

“Yes, Laine?”

“I thought it would be a good idea to let you be aware that I think I might possibly be capable of seeing past six feet. I am not quite sure, but I doubt I will need to look at Jimmy’s test answers anyway,” Laine said when he sat down in the nearest desk.

“I doubt he’ll even write any!” Tom pointed out, smirking.

Jimmy glared at Tom as if he was not sure how to respond. Tom responded to Jimmy by raising his eyebrows and smiling smugly. A split second after sitting down at his chosen desk, Laine jumped out of the seat, ready to lunge.

“Mrs. Duchamp?” I gestured.

"I'm on it," she said, already squelching a tenuous situation.

"OK," I said breathing out a sigh of relief, "Who else is here?"

"Mrs. Wright," Katie interrupted, "It's just the same old gang except for another freebee."

"That must be me? I am Annie. My teacher made me come. She said I cannot sit still, and it would be better if I had a nice quiet spot to practice sitting still in a chair. I told her that I am not used to sitting still. It is not in my nature – sitting still, that is. Do you make your students sit still? I do not want to do that. I have never practiced before. Should I go back to my class and practice sitting still?" Annie turned to leave.

"No, Annie," I said to her. "It is perfectly fine. You can practice sitting still here for today. I will talk to Mrs. Wells later."

"Nope," Katie interrupted, munching on a carrot as she ambled over to me. "Annie's teacher is Mrs. Williams. You really need to memorize who the teachers are in this school. My mom said old people start to lose their memory. I think you could be in that category. My grandma lives in a senior colony. I will have my mom tell you about it."

"Katie, why are you snacking already? We haven't even started the testing yet." I looked over at the snack table and saw Mrs. Duchamp covering up the contents with paper towels. "Mrs. Duchamp, would you kindly keep the children from eating the snacks."

Mrs. Duchamp finished what she was doing and, without turning her head toward me, said, "They tried to get the donuts and cookies, but I did a bait and switch."

Sam jumped up. "There are donuts here? No one told me about donuts. I should probably count them and make sure we didn't get short circuited."

There is enough food here to feed a small country, I said under my breath. Turning back to look down the hall for the others, I immediately noticed Herman. He was dressed for success. I always got a kick out of his outfits, which seemed to match his daily moods. Today, he had on a white, crisply starched shirt with a plaid vest and matching bow tie. Each trouser leg was pleated down the middle. He wore loafers from another era with checkered socks. I wondered where his mother found them, but I knew they often browsed in vintage shops. I also knew exactly what Herman would say and how he would say it because it was always the same.

"Good morning, Mrs. Wright. I am Herman H. Hilfinker the III, Junior. You can call me Junior. I believe I am here today to take another assessment. This one is called the WASL, which is the Washington Assessment of Student Learning. I am assuming that you have read the instructions fully and know what you are doing. Thank you. I will proceed to my desk now."

It was so easy to warm up to Herman. He had a pedantic, almost adult-like timbre in his voice as well as his spoken delivery. His teachers had never really been sure how to deal with his communication style, while most of the other students simply ignored it. Maybe they had a better understanding of it. No one really needed to know his specific diagnosis because he was just how he was. I actually found it quite charming.

"You can sit anywhere you like, Herman, I mean Junior."

"My desk is not where it should be. Have you discussed this with the principal? Is this on the stated requirements?"

"Yes, yes, it is. Thank you, Junior, for noticing."

"You are welcome, Mrs. Wright."

Katie put her head in her hands and shook it back and forth as she moaned loudly, "Oh for heaven's sake."

"Looks like that's everyone," I said. "I don't see anyone else down the hall."

"Look again!" Katie shook her head again. "Who are you forgetting, Mrs. Wright?"

Mrs. Duchamp looked at me with a knowing grin, saying, "It's Shane."

Tom twirled his pencil a few times before it dropped on the floor. "Shane is outside the boys' bathroom. He will not go in until the big hand on the hallway clock strikes 12 or 2. And no one can be in there. We may be here for all eternity."

"I'll get him," Sam said, jumping up and over his desk.

"No, that's very kind of you, but..."

"He wasn't being kind, Mrs. Wright," said Katie. "He's just trying to get out of here."

"I'll go get him. Mrs. Duchamp, will you please keep an eye on things? I'll be right back," I said without turning toward her.

"What?" Mrs. Duchamp replied.

CHAPTER 3

It's Only a Foot Away

I saw Shane as I walked swiftly and deliberately down the hallway and around the corner. I did not want to frighten him, so calling out his name would not be an option. He would not fear me. I knew that without any question or hesitation. I assumed he would be worried I might destroy his necessary routine. In my opinion, Shane was a unique and wonderful individual.

A few years earlier, we were all confused by Shane's unusual behavior. He was never a violent child, nor even a typical behaviorally disordered student. When his teacher had the students line up and walk down the hall, Shane would sometimes stop dead in his tracks and start screaming. He shook, stomped his feet, and hit his head repeatedly with his fists. All manner of asking him what was wrong and how we could help went unnoticed. I am not so sure he would have been able to explain even if he understood why this happened.

His family was also at a loss. They mentioned he used to do the same thing quite frequently at home but seemed to have grown out of it. They also told us he had a routine or a particular route he took when he went from one room to another.

I decided to monitor and observe Shane over a few weeks when his teacher told me the tantrums were getting worse. It did not take long to notice that Shane held out his arm so his fingertips could touch the wall. The teacher instructed all the students to keep their hands to themselves and walk in a straight line. When Shane could not feel the wall, he stopped and screamed. This happened if he was too close to the wall or too far away. I will never forget the day I gave him the pocket tape measure I kept in my purse for thrift store shopping. He turned his head slightly to one side and eyed the device.

"What is it for?" Shane asked.

"Watch me," I said. I pulled out the tape and measured from the tips of his fingers to his elbow. It was exactly twelve inches. I moved ahead of him a few steps and measured out another foot. "I am going to walk by staying the exact same distance from the wall."

Shane's eyes darted back and forth between the wall and the end of the tape measure. He did not move. His eyes found mine and he gave me the biggest smile I had ever seen.

"Now it is your turn," I said. "I will hold out the tape one foot from me to the wall. Come to me."

He did just that and instead of screaming, Shane jumped up and down with ecstatic joy. Over the next few years, the teachers became frustrated that his obsessive measuring and insistence on staying within one foot of the wall would take up so much time. Yet it did not take long until he figured out the route he needed to take to feel secure. I was hopeful that eventually we could fully phase out the measuring tape. The teachers were hoping that would be sooner than later. Sometimes he did not use it at all, but at times of anxiety for him, the measuring tape made a reappearance. Today was one of those times.

Shane was next to the boys' bathroom door. He looked so forlorn as he held out his measuring tape. As I was approaching, an older boy pushed open the bathroom door and knocked Shane out of the way. He stumbled backwards but did not say a word.

"Jessie!" I gave the offender my stern teacher look.

"Oh, sorry, Mrs. Wright. I didn't see you there."

"I think you must mean you didn't see Shane," I countered.

"Oh, no. I saw him."

I wanted to growl. Jessie glanced at my expression and turned toward Shane. "Oh, sorry, little guy," he said.

"I am not little. I am a fourth grader," Shane announced.

"Aren't you fourth graders supposed to be taking some weird test which is making all the teachers wacko about having to be quiet and all that?" Jessie added.

I put my hand lightly on Jessie's back and guided him in the direction of his classroom. "Thank you, Jessie, we are on our way to get started."

"I am fairly sure the other fourth grade classes started ages ago. You are way behind, Mrs. Wright. But I suppose that is not surprising," Jessie said as he started to walk back to his classroom.

Years of experience had taught me to hide my facial expressions of annoyance. I turned to Shane and said, "Let's go. The kids are waiting to take the test.

“He annoys you, huh, Mrs. Wright?”

CHAPTER 4

Some of My Brilliant Advice

When Shane and I reached the Resource Room, everyone was sitting at a desk and listening intently to a story Mrs. Duchamp was reading. If it had been in my power, my more than capable assistant would have made the same amount of money that I did. Which certainly wasn't much, but still more than she currently made. She did not get anywhere close to what she deserved.

"Hey!" Sam shouted. "It's about time you got here!"

I walked over to Mrs. Duchamp and whispered, "Thank you. Well done."

She smiled and let out a soft breath before saying, "In the nick of time. We better get started because it won't be long before recess."

"Recess? Good heavens," I said looking up at the clock. "That's in forty minutes. I won't have time to finish reading the directions by then."

Mrs. Duchamp and I turned around and bumped into Tom, who was standing directly behind us. "Do we even need directions? No one pays attention to them anyway. Seems like a waste of time to me. Maybe we should just cut through all of it and go directly to recess."

"How about you go directly to your seat?" I said, noticing a few others had left their desks and were roaming around the classroom.

"Excuse me, boys and girls," Mrs. Duchamp interrupted. "I don't remember saying you could leave your seats."

She is so good. I wish I had thought of that.

"Look, everyone," Jimmy said standing next to Shane. "Check out this T-shirt."

And just like that, the entire group flew out of their desks and surrounded Shane.

"Could you do that 'excuse me, boys and girls' thing again?" I said to Mrs. Duchamp.

"I don't get paid enough for this," she said with a smirk.

Jimmy pointed to Shane's T-shirt. "What does it say?"

Junior touched each word and read out loud as if he were the lead character actor center stage on Broadway. "I am who I am and nobody else."

"Wow, cool, that's awesome, I want a shirt like that," came the sounds from the other students. "Where did you get it?" someone else asked.

"My uncle George sent it to me for my birthday," Shane explained.

"I got a family crest for my birthday," Junior said.

Tom put his fingers on his forehead and massaged his temples. "Well, you got lucky. My grandma needs lessons on what to give her adoring grandson."

"Are you going to tell us what she got you or are you going to keep us waiting for all eternity?" Katie hissed.

"$1.37," Tom said.

"Excuse me, boys and girls," I tried. "Everyone go to your desk and sit down."

They all stared at me as if I had lost my mind. "Now!"

Mrs. Duchamp helped corral them back to their seats. I picked up the test booklets and the teacher instructions and walked deliberately to the front of the room. Out of the corner of my eye I saw one of my fifth graders leaning against the back wall. Oh, no, I thought. I said, "Matthew, what are you doing here?"

Without budging an inch, he surveyed the room and said, "Who's the new kid in my desk?"

Katie immediately left her desk and quickly moved in front of Annie. "That's Annie, and you are required to leave us this minute!"

"I can handle this. Thank you, Katie," I said.

"Just say the word and I've got this, Mrs. Wright. Old people don't move too fast, but I can," Katie said.

Matthew hissed at Katie before announcing, "This is my Math time, and I am supposed to come here for Math."

"Matthew," I said. "Today is the day we are giving the fourth graders the WASL test. Remember, we have been talking about it for weeks. I'm sure Mr. Baxter knows you are to stay in your regular classroom today."

"I think he might have been saying something to me when I sprinted out, but whatever he said got tangled in my ears."

"Tell Mr. Baxter that I sent you back."

"I can't go back there, Mrs. Wright. Please don't make me. They are doing Math. You know Math and I don't mix well."

"I have an idea," I said. "Take your Math packet from your cubby and work on that."

Matthew's eyes opened as wide as a hoot owl in the dark sky. "Tell me that's one of your weird jokes. The kids already think I am kind of stupid. If I go back with baby work, then they will know for sure that I am stupid."

"You are not stupid..." I tried to say but got cut off by Sam.

"Let me give you some of my brilliant advice," Sam said. "Just do what I do. Go back to class, lean back on your empty desk, and put your hands behind your head. When Mr. Baxter asks what you think you are doing, say that you had already completed the lesson they are currently doing when you were in the Resource Room. You are waiting until the others catch up with you and they can handle the more difficult stuff."

"Perfect, I am out of here!" Matthew said, rushing out the door.

"Mr. Baxter will be wise about that trick when you have him next year, Sam," I said, grinning.

"You wouldn't be so cruel as to put me in his class next year, would you, Mrs. Wright?"

"Let's see, is everyone sitting quietly at their desk ready to start now?" I asked.

All the students were in their seats, hands folded, and their eyes were on me. All was quiet. All was right in the Resource world – for the moment.

CHAPTER 5

Please Refrain from Asking Questions

Silence ensued without further ado. I always wanted to say that. Taking a deep breath, I looked at the clock and crossed my fingers behind my back.

"I saw that," Katie said, clearing her throat.

So much for a lengthy silence. It was time for me to exercise my zillion years in college. "The person who can stay the quietest the longest while I read the instructions will be the first one to go to the snack table during break time."

Hands were immediately folded again, and all eyes focused studiously on me. "This test direction teachers' guide looks a little lengthy to me," I said to Mrs. Duchamp. She tilted her head and only shrugged.

"Directions for Math Estimation, page one. I will hand out the test booklets when it states to do so in the directions." Oh, wait, I thought to myself. What are these sidebar boxes? "Notes to the teacher. Do not read these notes out loud." These boxes contained more information than the actual direction notes that were to be read to the students. I had a little idea of what it would say because we had received a few training sessions, but all after a long school day. I had not been paying a great deal of attention then. My thought was to read the teachers' guide ahead of time. Unfortunately, the teachers' guides were not distributed until the actual student tests arrived moments before the students came in.

I continued reading the test directions to the students verbatim. "It is very important that you use a number two pencil. You are not allowed to use a mechanical pencil or pen."

Laine and Annie raised their hands at the same time. Others looked their way and raised their hands as well.

I looked at the teacher box: "Students should refrain from asking questions until after all the instructions are given."

Should I actually say that to them? I looked toward Mrs. Duchamp, who was standing patiently at the back of the room. "Mrs. D, would you kindly look at your teachers' guide and give me your interpretation of when I can answer student questions about the directions?"

"I'm sorry, but I'm not able to," she said with a tight grin.

"Why ever not?" I asked.

"They only gave us one teachers' manual. Mrs. Williams said that she needed two manuals in case her coffee spilled on one. So, they took mine."

"You are a teacher in this classroom. You should have one, too," I said in a hushed whisper to her. She only shrugged.

"Why?"

I looked at all the students raising their hands. The "why" came from Laine, who was not one of my students.

"Please refrain from asking questions until I finish reading the directions," I read directly from the booklet. They put down their hands and I continued. Ten minutes later, another hand shot up at the same time Annie fell off her chair. She immediately scrambled back onto her chair and scooted close to her desk.

Jimmy ignored Annie but continued to wave one hand frantically while his other hand closed around his mouth. I could tell how much he wanted to win the snack bar no-talking contest.

"Please refrain from asking questions until I finish reading the directions."

He lost the contest. Jimmy's hand flew away from his mouth as if a gust of wind had forced the issue. "How am I supposed to wait to ask a question until you are done? I will forget it by then."

I looked at Mrs. Duchamp again, hoping she might be able to give me some expert guidance. She tilted her head and gave me what looked like an affirmative up and down movement. That was enough for me.

"What is your question, Jimmy?"

A long pause. An exceptionally long pause.

"Jimmy?" I asked again.

"I don't remember."

"I will continue. Please refrain from asking questions until I finish reading the directions. It is important to use a number two pencil. Do not use a mechanical pencil or pen." I wondered how many times they could possibly mention that pencil requirement.

"Why?" Annie asked this time.

"You already read that part, Mrs. Wright. Move on. I think it is getting dark in here. When do we go home?" Tom said.

Forty minutes did not exactly fly by, but the directions were finally over. Now, I could say what I had been dreading. "Are there any questions?"

A few hands shot up into the air.

"Yes, Sam?" Sam was the smartest boy in my class. He was full of energy and eager to discover new things. He never stopped asking questions that could excite or annoy any adult. He looked like a typical curious fourth grader. People were surprised he was a Special Education student when they saw him or heard him communicate. He appeared sharp beyond his years, but he struggled with written words. Sam could not read. He had hidden it so long by his high verbal vocabulary and continual use of distraction.

"I would like a clarification. Can you go back and read the part you said about twenty minutes ago?" Sam said.

I grimaced. Sometimes he was a little too cocky for his own good. Yet he always amused me. "I would be so happy to reread the entire directions booklet. Let's see, 'please use a number two pencil...'"

"My family uses special Hilfinker mechanical pencils. I believe I should have special dispensation. I believe it may be necessary for me to call my dad," Junior blurted out.

Sam only laughed. "I was wondering if you are going to read each question to us. All of us, I mean."

"Yes, Mrs. Duchamp and I will read each question to everyone except Laine, Annie, Junior, and Shane; however we are not allowed to give you any answers, hints, or help in any way."

Mixed voices of "that's not fair" erupted in the back of the room.

Herman H. Hilfinker the III, Junior, raised his hand and spoke quickly again without being acknowledged. "It has come to my immediate attention that I will need to proceed to the restroom facilities before I can assume test taking mode."

Tom shot up, "I couldn't have said it better and believe me I have tried. I want to go to the bathroom, too!"

"Tom and Junior," I said, "you had the opportunity to go when you walked down here earlier."

"Couldn't," Tom said, "Shane was in the way. I was afraid he was going to measure the stalls or something."

"You don't know anything!" Shane said. "The tape measure is only for the hallway walls. You need to be a little more observant."

I looked through the teachers' directions, trying to remember the bathroom break instructions. I almost shouted with glee as I read aloud, "Students may have a five-minute bathroom break after the directions are read and before testing commences."

The kids gave a mild cheer and quickly dashed out of their desks.

"Wait, wait, everyone," I said. "Here are the rules – you are to walk down the hallway quickly but quietly. I do not want to hear one word or sound. You are to go to the bathroom and come back here directly. You are not allowed to wander off anywhere else. Do you understand?"

"Yes," Mrs. Wright," they all chorused.

Mrs. Duchamp followed the students in her exemplary supervision role. I stayed behind to supervise the testing booklets.

CHAPTER 6

Two More Trespassers

It was not long before I heard the scuffling sound of returning footsteps. I could also clearly hear Katie telling Mrs. Duchamp that she observed lines in her hair as if someone used a gray crayon. When they entered the classroom, Mrs. Duchamp came to me and whispered, "Katie intends to ask her mother if they can find us a double room at the senior colony!"

I watched as each student and another two extras entered the room.

"We have new additions," Katie blurted out as she stormed through the doorway and into the classroom like a whirlwind tumbleweed finding its path down an empty street.

"I'm Brant and this is Kerry. Our teacher, Mrs. Haggart, didn't want us around anymore."

"Oh, no," Katie said. "Throw them out, Mrs. Wright. We don't want the regulars to find out about our secrets. They are trespassing. I am going to file a complaint!"

"I agree," chorused everyone else in the room, including the other two general education students.

"Alright, but they will need to stay and take the test for now. I will talk to Mrs. Haggart later. Sit down at those desks in the back row."

Sam's head flew around to the back desks and back toward me before saying, "Hey, I tried to sit in the back row so you wouldn't notice me, but you refused. That is not fair. How come those regulars can do whatever they want, and your very own students cannot?"

"So, Brant and Kerry," I continued, ignoring Sam, "Why are you showing up now instead of earlier when the instructions were given?"

"Heard the instructions, Mrs. Wright. That's when Mrs. Haggart said we were too smart to take the test," Kerry said.

Brant shuffled his feet and looked away. "Actually, she said we were a couple of smart alecks. She called the principal, who came down and sent us here. So, after Mrs. Schultz stomped off in a huff, we headed down here."

Kerry elbowed Brant and held his head up high. "We couldn't pass the gym without a quick look inside to see if there was any action going on. Since no one was there, it seemed like a good idea to have a bit of one on one. Not our fault Mr. Sonic, the PE teacher, left the basketballs out."

"Just our luck that Mrs. Schultz wanted to check out the gym at the same time," Brant added, biting his nails.

Kerry's eyes darted around the room as if hoping for some camaraderie from his fellow schoolmates. "We only asked if she wanted to join us in a quick game."

"We did say quick," Brant added.

"I wish you hadn't added the fact that she could certainly use the exercise because she was a bit roly-poly," Kerry said. "Mrs. Schultz's face got even redder than it usually is."

Brant only sighed and said, "Well, everyone knows it's true. Then she asked us our names."

"I told her my name was Tom."

"I told her my name was Sam," Brant said, "and we were on our way to the Resource Room just like she advised us."

The class erupted in laughter, except for Mrs. Duchamp and me.

"I happened to also mention that we go here every single day," Kerry said. "I thought it would help the situation."

The kids laughed even louder.

"You two are dumb as a box of rocks!" Tom exclaimed.

I looked around the room with my most stern teacher expression plastered onto my face. "Tom!" I glared at him. "You know how I feel about name calling. That is absolutely enough!"

Sam had tears rolling down his face from laughing hysterically. "Mrs. Wright, you have to see how funny those fools are! Mrs. Schultz knows Tom and me and everyone else who comes to the Resource Room. She is here all the time. Well, maybe not all the time."

"More than I care to see her," Shane said under his breath as he reorganized his number two pencils and the math manipulatives on his desk.

Tom shook his head. "My mom said if she has to go to one more conference this year, she will scream. She told me that the principal is always there. I think it might make her a little nervous."

Now the only students not laughing were Brant and Kerry. "Go sit down, boys, and we will talk about this later with Mrs. Schultz," I said.

"Do we have to?" Brant said when he sat down. He started chewing on his number two pencil as soon as Mrs. Duchamp put it on his desk.

Sam turned around to face Brant and Kerry and said, "Not so smart now, are you? You are always telling everyone that it is only the dummies who go to the Resource Room. Well, welcome home."

"Looks like you'll be doing a lot of talking to staff during the recess break," Mrs. Duchamp said as she passed me to take two test booklets to our newcomers.

As if on cue, the recess bell shrilled, giving me and most of the kids a bit of a fright.

Junior looked around as if he was trying to figure out where the sound came from. "I believe the decibel level of the recess alarm needs to be toned down," he said.

I am not sure why it surprised me, but all the students stayed at their desks and waited until I dismissed them. I did enjoy conditioned responses. Feeling a bit relieved myself, I said, "You may go to recess in just a moment. Please remember instruction #29B. You are not to talk about the test to anyone. You cannot ask anyone any questions or tell anyone about the test. You cannot tell anyone what the questions were or what answers you gave. Is that understood?"

A few hands went up. "Yes, Annie," I said.

"We haven't started the actual test yet, Mrs. Wright. Or did you forget that?"

"She forgot," Katie answered.

"Everyone is dismissed. When the bell rings, please come directly back here and not to your regular classroom. Sit down quietly and we will begin."

The room was eerily still once all the kids had left. Mrs. Duchamp and I plopped down onto the closest chairs and breathed a sigh of relief.

"Want a nice cup of hot tea? Lemon and one sweetener?" Mrs. Duchamp asked.

"Yes, absolutely. Can that be put permanently in your job description?"

"Don't press your luck."

CHAPTER 7

Eyes Widely Shut

The end of recess exploded in my head with the shriek of the bell. I jumped in unexpected terror as hot tea spilled down the front of my dress, leaving a trail of wet residue like a flash flood on a dry clay hillside.

"Why doesn't this ever happen to you?" I asked Mrs. Duchamp as I tried to blot stains with the tiny tissue she gave me.

"I don't drink tea," she answered, heading to the back door.

"Grmpf," came the guttural noises from Mrs. Schultz, the principal. I felt like I was jumping out of my skin a second time. Why did she like to sneak inside instead of announcing that she was on her way to bother me? Mrs. Schultz cleared her voice once more before escorting Brant and Kerry into the classroom while tugging on the necklines of their shirts. "These miscreants claim they belong to you!"

"I suppose they do," I said, "for today anyway."

"Keep them in here then. They never seem to be where they are supposed to be. And they are sopping wet."

"Maybe us fragile children shouldn't be sent out in a torrential downpour," Brant said, glaring at the principal.

"And maybe YOU TWO shouldn't be climbing wet trees!" She glared back at them, then, swiftly turning her focus directly toward me, said, "Where are the rest of your students? Why aren't you testing them? The other classes are almost done."

"They should be returning from recess any moment," I said.

"Recess was over three minutes ago. Everyone is back in their classes silently observing the rules of testing protocol," Mrs. Schultz said, her face apparently ready to explode into a shade of scarlet.

I am not sure why, but principals had never intimidated me. They seemed to come and go like a revolving door, which meant that I was expected to adjust to each new personality and each new educational philosophy. Eventually, I usually managed to coax them around to accepting my unique teaching methods. Sometimes they just annoyed me. I never thought I had a lot of patience, yet for some odd reason people often thought Special Education teachers had a reservoir of never-ending patience. I did not. Mrs. Duchamp, on the other hand, had tons. I opened my mouth to respond to Mrs. Schultz, unsure what to say, when I realized that my ever-faithful aide had disappeared.

Mrs. Duchamp poked her head around the doorway and directed her comments to the principal. "Our students are waiting quietly around the corner. They did not want to unnecessarily interrupt your important conversation with Mrs. Wright. Shall I bring them in now? They are eager to commence testing."

Mrs. Schultz looked as if she had swallowed something sour. She nodded her head and turned to me. "How long until you are done?"

"We have to read each question to most of the Resource students and that can take quite a bit of time," I answered.

"I can be done in five seconds flat if you want me to, Mrs. Schultz," Tom said as he walked swiftly to his desk and sat down.

"That won't be necessary, Tom. You are Tom, aren't you?"

"I could say that I am Brant?" Tom grinned.

"Hrmpf!" Mrs. Schultz left without another word or sound.

Mrs. Duchamp put her hands on her hips and addressed the class, "Excuse me, boys and girls, I remember you were told to come straight back here and not to your regular classrooms. Your teachers were not happy when I went to collect you."

"Sorry," came the chorused reply.

I mouthed my apology and appreciative thanks to Mrs. Duchamp before addressing the students. "Are you sitting comfortably?" I asked. "Then I shall begin."

"You always say that when you are going to read a story," Jimmy said. "I'm not sure Math is in that category. You could get us confused."

"I'm not confused," Laine said.

Tom dropped another pencil and leaned over to pick it up while saying, "If Lame is not confused, then neither am I."

Laine glared at Tom. "My name is Laine, not Lame!"

"Oh, is it? Sometimes I get confused," Tom said turning his head toward me while smiling widely.

I gave Tom the "knock it off" look and continued, "Then we shall begin. Please open your test booklets to page one. Follow along as I read the instructions out loud."

"More instructions?" Katie's moaning clearly reflected how I felt but could not say.

"Remember to use only a number two pencil. Mechanical pencils or pens are not allowed."

"This is highly discriminatory," Junior announced. "I still say my famous Hilfinker engraved mechanical pencil should be among my use of tools for this particular assessment. My dad is going to make you put it in my IEP."

"What's an IEP?" Brant looked up from his booklet. "Can I have one, too?"

I put my finger to my lips to gesture silence. Both boys immediately put a hand over their mouths.

The room was surprisingly silent as I gazed in wonder at everyone sitting at attention. The general education students were sitting at the back of the room while those of my students who receive specially designed instruction in Reading in the Resource Room were gathered in a small group with appropriate distancing up front because Mrs. Duchamp and I were required to read them the test questions. My assistant looked at me and nodded her head that she was ready. I nodded back. Here we go, I thought to myself, closing my eyes for a brief moment.

CHAPTER 8

The Paper Explosion

"Laine?" I said, gasping, my eyes now wide open. I focused directly on our so-called new student. As if a thought bubble had exploded in my head, I knew instantly who Laine was and why he was in our room. Mrs. Duchamp must have realized it at the same time. She got up and went straight to the wall phone. "I am assuming you are calling the office?" I asked. She only nodded and handed me the receiver.

"Yes, hi, Doris. Are there large-print test...?" I tried to ask, speaking directly into the phone, but she anticipated exactly what I wanted and spoke without missing a beat. "Yes, please send someone down here. Yes, all of it. We will organize it. No, we cannot get it ourselves. Yes, OK. I suppose one of the naughty boys can bring it down. No, please do not send two or three boys. One is enough. Thank you, Doris. We appreciate it." Mrs. Duchamp nodded her head at me again as I hung up the phone. She turned around and headed straight to Laine's desk and whispered something in his ear. Laine's head jolted up off the table.

Katie looked at Laine and back to me. "I thought he was smelling his desk, but now it makes more sense after that private call you allowed us to listen in on.

Laine looked around at all the eyes staring at him and said without embarrassment, "My mom says I must have large print. She thinks I will do better, but if you gave me one of those gigantic I-spy glasses that detectives use, I would be fine. Things are a tiny bit blurry sometimes."

I was the one embarrassed as I had forgotten about Laine's vision impairment. I was afraid Katie would convince me my upcoming dementia was setting in. Laine's disability had been identified but was not severe enough to warrant specially designed instruction in a Resource Room. He was an average student academically and only needed some special accommodations occasionally. Students like Laine often had what we called a 504 plan. It was not an individualized educational plan (IEP), but it did specify what the child needed to maintain appropriate instruction in the general education classroom. I had had to order large-print testing materials weeks ago. Unfortunately, I forgot to get it with my other supplies before testing started. Of course, it would have been nice if someone in the office had told me it had come in.

All heads seemed to swirl at once away from Laine and toward the open doorway as a tiny voice squeaked behind a pending avalanche of wobbling papers. "Where do you want these?"

Mrs. Duchamp and I jumped up simultaneously and raced to catch the papers as they fell and scattered every which way onto the floor like fallen tree leaves during a sudden whirlwind on a brisk autumn day. The little boy dropped to his bottom and was entirely hidden in the mound of large-print test papers.

"You don't want me to help with that, do you, Mrs. Wright?" Tom said, grinning widely.

"No, no. Everyone, please go back to your tests and start the first problem. We can handle this," I said and added, "I think."

"We can't start because you have insisted that we are not allowed to read it by ourselves." Tom smiled impishly. "I'm happy to wait. This paper explosion is much more entertaining."

Katie peered at Tom and said, "About time you actually said something that makes sense. You know, I'm beginning to think we should do this WASL every day."

"I'm up for that," said Brant. "Can Kerry and I come, too?"

Kerry looked at Brant with confused creases drawn on his forehead. "Well, maybe not every day. I'm thinking we could stay in our real class when there is a movie or party, or Mrs. Haggart is snoring at her desk.

As I had fallen to my knees in hopes of catching a few of the flying poster-sized test pages, I couldn't help but giggle. Mrs. Duchamp suppressed a wave of uncontrollable laughter, but I knew she was close to losing it. Her lips were held tightly closed and squeezed in by her teeth. I looked up at her and said, "I have this faint memory of hanging huge white sheets on a laundry line outside our log house on a very brisk and windy day. I was so small. I remember being wrapped up in them and tumbling over and down a small hill."

Mrs. D sank to the floor, her mouth flying open as a gale of laughter escaped uncontrollably. Everyone in the room broke into simultaneous giggles and expressions of mirth. We gathered up the papers and tried to organize them as best we could. As the room started to quiet down, we noticed Laine trying to help the small child who was sitting cross legged on the floor with a few papers still clinging to him. Laine managed to pull the child up without much effort and said so all could hear, "You know, this is all my mother's idea. Why don't I just put my glasses on?"

A squeaky voice rang out, "Mrs. Wright, should I go get the rest of these test papers now?"

"Is it snack time yet?" Jimmy asked no one in particular.

"No," I answered calmly and without rancor while taking on the challenge of a drill sergeant. "Brant and Kerry and Annie, open your booklets and start on page one. You, too, Junior and Shane, because even though you come into the Resource Room, I can't read the questions to you. Your goals are not in Reading."

"I find this increasingly difficult to absorb the necessity of reading to some but not all, but if you insist I shall..." Junior started but didn't finish his comments when I interrupted him.

I turned to everyone, ready to give a dramatic speech. "This is not a courtroom. There will be absolutely no talking. Tom, Sam, Katie, and Jimmy, open to page one and wait as Mrs. Duchamp will come around and start reading the first question to you. I will put Laine's test pages in order on his desk, then I will come help as well."

"Mrs. Wright," Katie announced in her best dramatic version of authority, "You should probably focus some attention on Shane. He has his tape measure out and looks like he is ready to do some Math measurements that are not in the test."

"You don't know anything, Katie," Shane said, not looking at anyone. "I don't come here for Reading so I am trying to figure out where I should really be sitting."

"I've got this," Mrs. Duchamp said while moving Shane's desk an appropriate distance away from Junior's desk.

"Mrs. D, let's move my desk back there, too, because I feel I am perfectly capable of read..." Katie started to say but stopped abruptly when she saw my expression.

Everyone seemed to be watching and waiting for my reaction but did exactly as they were told. I couldn't help but smile inside and breathe a sigh of exasperation. Mrs. Duchamp was an expert at swiftly and competently reading any situation that came up.

On the other hand, I had a few silent swear words swimming in my head as I struggled to figure out the numerical order of the gigantic papers. As soon as I put a few down, the others would cascade off the desk and I would start all over again.

Laine whispered in my ear, "I have an idea, Mrs. Wright."

"I'm listening."

"See the numbers at the bottom. I think those are numbers. They could be letters or animal figures for all I can tell, but maybe put them in chronological order on the big table over there and hand me them one at a time."

"You are one smart boy. OK, page ONE," I said as I put the first page, which had maybe one or two sentences, down on his desk. The test paper immediately extended beyond all sides of the rectangular desk and Laine scrambled to grab it before his special test could tumble to the floor. "When you finish one, put it on the floor and I will bring the next one."

I went over to help Mrs. Duchamp, but immediately flew back to Laine's desk. He was fast and I was way too slow. It was going to be a long day.

CHAPTER 9

Dogs and Cats

I looked at Mrs. Duchamp as she nodded back at me. Four desks were swiftly moved into a semi-circle formation, enabling Tom, Katie, Sam, and Jimmy to face me and listen intently as I read each math question to them. Mrs. Duchamp moved swiftly over toward Laine and the other students. We smiled weakly at each other and took over our respective roles.

"One, two, three, look at me," I announced with my best teacher exuberance.

Katie looked at the newly assembled group and rolled her eyes. "So, this must be the new Math testing opening remarks."

I glanced quickly at Katie and smiled, "Katie, please double wrap a screen around your thoughts and..."

"What is that supposed to mean?" she jumped in before I could finish.

"It might have something to do with the Reading test we took last week," Tom remarked without looking up.

"Metaphor or simile or analogy or something we were forced to memorize a thousand times this year in preparation for this dumb test," Sam cut in.

Jimmy shrugged his shoulders and said, "I only want to learn how to read; then Mrs. Wright wouldn't have to read this unintelligible test to me."

Herman H. Hilfinker the III, Junior, stood up as if he were a soldier at attention ready to salute. "That brings up an excellent point of discussion before we all must commence with this travesty."

"Junior," I scolded, "Please resume your testing independently so I can quietly read the questions to our students who come to the Resource Room for Reading instruction. You don't come in here for Reading and must take the Math test without reading assistance."

"I am well aware of that, Mrs. Wright. And you have indicated that numerous times, although I believe we should thoroughly examine the particular adjustments for readers versus non-readers and the implications therein," he said.

"Would everyone like me to recite the ten-page directions once again?" I asked the group as a whole.

"No!" came the unified response.

I ambled toward Junior and whispered, "I believe that sounds like a very feasible idea. Let's discuss this at your parents' conference tomorrow."

Junior plopped back down on his chair and picked up his number two pencil without another word.

Returning to my group, I overheard a hushed argument about never having heard the word metaphor before. Jimmy growled at his testing companions. "It is just not fair to even hear that word right now when our brains are to be focused on Math today, not reading."

"One, two, three, look at me." I quickly opened my eyes wide toward Katie while putting one forefinger to my lips, making the universal silence gesture.

After whispering the first question to my four students, I looked up and noticed everyone in the class staring at me. Even those in the back of the room who were supposed to be reading and taking the test without assistance were focused on me.

Tommy raised his hand. "Mrs. Wright, I am not a dog."

Even Katie nodded. I was completely baffled no one found that statement odd except me. Even Mrs. Duchamp turned to gaze at us.

"Tommy?" I questioned.

"Mrs. Wright," Sammy interrupted, answering for Tom, "Only dogs would be able to hear your mumblings."

"My grandma, who is old like you, said dogs hear one thousand times more than humans," Katie said.

"You mean smell." Tom looked at Katie and wrinkled his nose.

"I do not smell!"

Annie jumped up and out of her chair, which tumbled noisily over, causing her test booklet to skid across the room. As Mrs. Duchamp quickly gathered the papers and set the chair and desk upright, Annie said, "My dog smells when he gets back from the spa. My mom always complains that the smell makes me a little hyper."

Kerry looked up and said to her, "Did they use that stinky peppermint perfume stuff? My dog spa did that and he smelled like a girl dog for a week. He was too embarrassed to play with his dog friends."

"I prefer cats," Brant said, jumping into the cat and dog debate.

"It is so true," Sammy added. "My grandpa said dogs can smell one thousand times more than people."

"Maybe we should test that assumption for our next Science Fair project," Junior said, without jumping to attention this time.

"Boys and girls," I announced again using my best teacher voice and wide eye movements. "One, two, three, look at me."

Katie looked around to everyone and grinned sheepishly, "Math. Get it?"

Exhaling loudly, I continued, "Front of class, you will be the clever dogs who listen intently and obey every command. Back of class, you will be the smart cats who work independently and silently while ignoring everything around them."

Mrs. Duchamp and I walked back to our stations impressed with the fresh stillness of our classroom. Before she sat down, she squeezed my arms. "OK, question number two coming up."

I sat down and rapidly jumped right back up when Mrs. Duchamp squealed, "Oh, no!"

CHAPTER 10

Measurement Made Easy

"Oh, no," I replied back. "There's a dog question coming up!"

"Don't get ahead of yourself, Mrs. Wright. We haven't finished the last one," Tom added. "But that's OK. I don't mind skipping it."

"I am ready for you to read the next one," Jimmy shouted as he waved his hand wildly in the air.

Tom looked around, probably hoping other students would be paying attention to him. "Mrs. Wright is all about dogs. It wouldn't be wise to disappoint her."

"Jimmy and Tom," I said, shifting my focus to both boys. "There is no need for any loud noises or any noise for that matter. I am sitting right in front of you. I can see your hand raised, Jimmy," I said, trying not to sound exasperated. "Except for your hand, Tommy."

Tommy raised his eyebrows and stared back at me. "That is because I need my hand for writing, if I were to write that is."

Jimmy shifted in his seat and continued to bob his hand up and down.

"Ok, Jimmy, what is it? Quietly please."

Jimmy gazed at me and shrugged. "My mind was flooded with thoughts that I would fail if you didn't pay attention to me."

"I'm paying attention now. Please remember that I can read the Math problems, but I can't answer any questions," I said with sympathy dripping from my voice.

"Do I write N, S, E, W?" Jimmy asked, totally ignoring my pleas.

"Just do the best you can," I said again.

"Or maybe they want me to write the complete words – North, South, East, West?"

"Whatever you think."

"How am I supposed to know? Was that explained in the directions? I was thinking about recess and didn't really pay attention. You should have told me to pay attention. This is important stuff. Now I don't know what to do."

"You can do this. Let's go to the next one and you can come back to this one later," I said.

With a defiant cross of his arms, Jimmy said, "No! I have to do this or nothing at all!"

So, I read the question again. Jimmy put both hands on his head and moaned. "Do I draw a flight plan or the plane?"

"I can read the problem once more, but I can't help you with the answer," I repeated.

"I don't get it. What should I write?"

Luckily I was given a reprieve by Laine frantically waving his hand while at the same time focusing intently on his huge test paper. "Sorry, Jimmy," I said, "I need to help Laine momentarily."

"Fine, just ignore me and go help your non-student," Jimmy said.

"*Do I detect the sound of a martyr burning*," I thought to myself, paraphrasing a John Cleese line.

"It doesn't make sense," Laine said when I reached him.

"Maybe he needs larger print," Katie said, shaking her head.

"Laine is right. This next question doesn't make sense. It can't be answered," Brant yelled from across the room.

"You better read it quickly, Mrs. Wright," Tom suggested.

I looked at Mrs. Duchamp and she sighed back at me. I returned to the test question and read it in a semi-whisper. "If a flea hops one inch at a time on a dog that is 3 feet in length, how many inches would it take to get to its tail?"

Tom crinkled his forehead and said in a whisper so loud that I was sure he could be heard down the hall, "That's easy. It would never get there because the dog would eat it!"

I noticed a number of students nodding their heads and scribbling quickly. But due to testing restrictions, I was powerless to question their responses in any way, including odd facial expressions, which Katie believes I practice daily in the mirror.

"Next question. Everyone, please read the question silently to yourself as I whisper it aloud to the students sitting around me," I said again.

Katie glared at me, "Oh, Mrs. Wright, how are Annie and I ever supposed to concentrate when you talk so much?"

"I am concentrating really well. I haven't fallen out of my desk since recess and I am keeping track for my mom,"

Annie said, bouncing off her chair and landing bottom up on the floor. Her chair, test booklet, two number two pencils, calculator, straight edge and/or ruler, and exactly two 8 by 10–inch scratch papers landed on top of her. "Does this time count?"

"Next question," I continued. "Your teacher's coat closet measures 8 feet high, 3 feet in width, and 4 feet in depth. What is the volume of the closet?"

Shane gently put his number two pencil down and smiled toward me. "So, they tried to pull a fast one on me, but they failed. I know this one."

"Everyone, please work on this problem until I return from helping Shane," I said to my assembled test takers.

"I don't think he needs help. He said he knew the answer," Katie responded.

I walked over to Shane and squatted down beside his desk. "That is wonderful, Shane," I said with a genuine smile that spread wide as I turned my head toward Mrs. Duchamp. I was surprised, however, when she didn't appear to be smiling back.

"It can't be answered," Shane's words echoed into my confused brain.

"The directions indicate that you are allowed to use a calculator," I suggested.

"Why?"

"So, you can calculate the answer."

"Why? This is not like the distance to a wall that requires obvious measurement."

"This is a different kind of measurement."

“There is no answer,” Shane said. “So, I will leave it blank. I am positive that is the correct response.

Junior looked over at us, straightened his tie, and wrote, “It is impossible to surmise a reasonable calculation to this apparently inane question.”

I looked at both of them. “Here are your calculators. Use them.”

“It won’t be necessary,” Shane said.

“Why not?” I finally asked in a strained whisper.

Shane looked at me, an incredulous annoyance spreading over his face, “No one is allowed in your closet. It is locked.”

“I’ve been in it!” Katie jumped in.

“When? Did you hide in there? Did you take measurements?” Tom asked in his loud whispering technique. He was out of his seat and at Shane’s desk before Mrs. Duchamp and I could turn around.

“Tom!” I said in a bit of a shrill voice. “You need to immediately go back to your desk. And Katie, please do not talk to Shane.”

“Okay, I will talk to Tom instead,” Katie quickly responded. “I wasn’t hiding in the closet, but I checked it out when Mrs. Wright told me to go to her desk and wait for her. She might have been under the wrong impression that I wasn’t behaving. Since she was taking all eternity to get there, I tried out the closet door.”

“What were the exact dimensions of the enclosed space?” Junior asked.

“No idea because Mrs. Wright chose that moment to sprint toward me,” Katie continued.

I must have been at a loss for words because when I opened my mouth to regain control, nothing came out.

Junior addressed his new captive audience, "Even if someone managed to sneak into said closet with an appropriate measurement tool, these specific numbers on this question are obviously wrong."

"Exactly," Shane said.

Mrs. D. and I stared at each other in obvious confusion. Call it a lapse of judgement on my part, but I couldn't help it. "I have to know. Why do you think these numbers are incorrect?" I asked.

Herman, Shane, Tom, and Katie laughed. Jimmy and Sam joined in by giggling. Then everyone else in the room did the same except for the two stunned teachers.

"You can take the honors, Katie," Junior said with an impish grin.

"Mrs. Wright, you must realize that the closet would not meet the eight-foot standard height. If it did, you would never be able to hang your coat in there. You would not be able to reach it."

"Thereby, we must assume that this is a trick question," Junior added, while Shane nodded vigorously.

"No wonder she keeps it locked. Or maybe that is why she uses the coatrack by the front door," Tom said to no one in particular.

I pulled a chair between Shane and Junior and sat down while rubbing my forehead with my fingertips and massaging my temples with my thumbs. I looked over at Mrs. Duchamp and sighed when I noticed she was already sitting in front of the group reading the next question to them.

"I think I'm going to throw up!" Jimmy cried.

CHAPTER 11

To Snack or To Test – Is That a Question?

"Just don't throw up on the WASL test booklet!" I said, trying not to sound as if I was pleading. The groan was only a silent rumble in my head. "And everyone, please remember the rule about silence during testing."

Katie stared at me but voiced her obvious displeasure to Mrs. Duchamp. "Mrs. Wright is not following the rules."

With astute confidence, Mrs. Duchamp put her finger under the next question and refocused Katie and the others. Two minutes of glorious silence followed until Shane frantically waved his hand and gestured me toward him. "Yes, Shane?" I said, smiling.

"Is that a question?" he asks. "This problem says to write a question. Is that a question? How do I write a question about Math? This isn't supposed to be a writing test."

"I can read the question to you, but I can't help you with the question," I answered.

"So, you can't tell me a question?" Shane asks again.

"Just do your best."

Nothing.

"Do you want to go to the next one?"

"Is that a question?" Shane asks hopefully.

Over by Mrs. Duchamp's group I could see Jimmy lift his head up. In a tiny voice he said to those around him, "I threw up eating lunch yesterday. Just thinking about food is making my stomach twirl."

"When is snack time?" Katie added.

I strolled over to those students and whispered, "Just think about what you are doing on the test."

"What if it is about food? Should I just throw up on the test or run out of the room?"

"Since Mrs. Duchamp is sitting by your desk, just tell her."

I am not quite sure, but Mrs. Duchamp might have given me an icy glare. She stood up and motioned me over toward a quiet, non-student area. She turned her back away from the students watching us and said to me, "This might be a good time for a snack break. I think the kids may be getting on your final nerve."

We turned as one to face our students. "OK, everyone, please close your Math Estimation test booklets and turn them over."

Sammy looked baffled. "This whole thing is about Math Estimation? We've never done Math Estimation. I don't even know what Math Estimation is. Why am I doing a test on Math Estimation when I don't know what Math Estimation is?"

Katie huffed loudly and said in her most annoyed voice possible, "That is all Mrs. Wright talked about for the past six weeks, Sam! Math Estimation is when..."

"Katie," I cut in quickly, "You are not to talk about the test!"

"What's the difference?" Katie adds. "He never pays attention anyway."

"Oh, like you do?" Sammy argued back.

"If everyone would like a break at the snack table, you two will need to be kind to each other."

All the students turned toward the two miscreants and glowered.

"Fine," they whimpered in unison.

Jimmy shouted out again, "Mrs. Wright, I'm not kidding this time. I have to go to the bathroom or maybe throw up. I'm not sure, but it is one of those."

"Well, OK, everyone. Let's take our break now. It has been 42 minutes since we started session II of the Math Estimation test, not counting the required rules and directions. I guess we can take a tiny break now," I said looking at my notes and ignoring the groans around the room. "Oh wait, there's more. It looks like you can't have lunch or go to the bathroom until Part II-B, exercise 7, is completely done."

"I'm done!" yelled Tom.

"Tom, we haven't started that part yet," I replied.

"Mrs. Wright, quit talking so much. I've got to go. I'm fidgeting over here," Sam said. "I gotta get to the bathroom fast!"

"And this throw-up is trying to escape out of my throat!" Jimmy whined.

The groaning in the room must have been coming from me. "OK, OK. You two can go across the hall into the bathroom. I can monitor you by sight if I use a mirror and slant it at a particular angle. Now where is a mirror?"

"Mrs. Wright, is that is a Math question?" asked Shane.

Jimmy and Sammy jumped out of their chairs and flew out of the classroom door. Everyone else immediately tried to do the same. "Wait, wait, stop! Not everyone all at once. Sam and Jimmy can go first. Everyone else can make a nice orderly line to the banquet table for snacks. And remember, no one is to talk about the test or your answers," I said, ignoring the rumbling and grumbling.

"Mrs. Duchamp, will you please see what snacks we were given for a small treat?"

She looked at the three-table spread she had set up and said, "You can have grapes or bananas or cookies, celery and carrots, pretzels and cheese goldfish crackers or regular crackers or graham crackers, vanilla wafers, orange slices, cheese sticks, cheese and cracker sandwiches, apple wedges, with or without peanut butter, various granola and healthy type bars that I am sure won't be touched, and there are a few donuts left. Oh, and water. I haven't had this much food in a week."

"I know," I said directed to her alone. "At the third WASL training session – or was it the fifth, I can't remember now –they implied it was crucial to provide students with nourishment."

"And ten extra pounds!"

"Where's the candy?" Annie asked. "My dad says I am a whirling dervish and maybe I should have more candy. My mom told him that he was being facetious, and he needed to stop confusing me. They had an argument, but it was me who was sent to bed. I have no idea what they were talking about, and I still don't understand why I got removed from a conversation that was about me."

"Can I have gum?" Shane looked ruefully around the snack table. "I can't concentrate without gum. My IEP says that I'm supposed to have gum when I work."

"When have you ever worked?" Katie exclaimed irritably. "If he gets gum, then I should get gum, too. I am not working without gum!"

"Oh, sure. Like you ever worked!" Shane hissed back at her.

I broke in at the nick of time. "Listen, no more talk about gum. There are plenty of snacks here."

"I am telling my mom you didn't follow the IEP...what's an IEP?" Shane asked.

"Mrs. Duchamp, have Sam and Jimmy come back yet?" I asked.

"I don't know, but I wasn't able to find the mirror to watch them," she answered.

"I'll go get them," Katie said as she rushed out the door.

"NO!" But it was too late. Katie was out of sight, with or without the spying mirror.

I gave up that fight and turned to face the other students. "OK, everyone, time to finish up your snacks and go...Shane, stop! Don't eat that grape next to your test! Go back to the snack table!"

"Is there gum there?" he asked, returning to the table. "And going back and forth is kind of confusing me before we continue with the next part of the test. Without gum, I will be totally confused. Maybe I will think it is a Writing test instead of a Math test. Do you want that on your conscience, Mrs. Wright?"

Sam and Jimmy rushed back into the classroom and straight toward the snack table as if it was the finishing line of their personal racetrack. Panting heavily, Jimmy said, "Mrs. Wright, our real teacher, said that you were not supposed to send us back to our class until we were completely through with the test and that should be the entire day. She doesn't want us back."

Sam added, "You are in trouble, Mrs. Wright. Our teacher didn't look very happy."

At that moment, Katie rushed back in and shouted, "I'm telling! Mrs. Wright, Sam and Jimmy were talking about the test!"

"Were not!"

"Were too!"

"You are such a tattletale!"

Katie gave the two boys her best scowl and turned her head to focus on me. "Jimmy asked Sam what he thought of the Writing test. Sam said that it wasn't a Writing test, it was a Math test. Jimmy said it looked like a Writing test to him because all he was supposed to do was write. Sam asked him what he thought of the money question, but Jimmy didn't even know it had money. And they were running in the hall and jumping up to touch the top of the wall. The custodian hates that! Can I go tell the principal?"

"Sit down, Katie. Sit down everyone. Toss the snacks and go back to your desks."

Shane froze. "I can't! I have to finish everything on my paper plate. People are starving in the world. I'm sure if I don't finish it, I'll starve, I'm telling my mom that you made me starve. Can I call my mom?"

I looked around in confusion, focusing only on an unusual sound. "What's that noise?" I was so used to hearing the droning of the rain that everything else faded into the background.

Katie slid up quietly behind me with a large donut stuffed into her mouth. I was a bit startled and jumped when she mumbled, "It's the melodic tinkle of what is supposed to be a lunch bell tune."

"Lunch bell? We've never had a bell for lunch before."

"My teacher said it is just during testing," Katie added. "When I was spying earlier after recess, I accidentally overheard a bunch of teachers arguing about the loud morning bell. They didn't seem really happy when they eventually noticed I was in the middle of their little pow wow group. Luckily, Mrs. D. rescued me in the nick of time."

"I think it could very possibly be for the teachers in case they fall asleep while making us suffer through this testing and forget to watch the clock, thereby causing us hungry children to forgo our scheduled mealtime," Junior said to everyone.

Tom gazed at me, sorrow outlining his expression. "This could be specifically for you, Mrs. Wright. You have to admit that it is kind of weird to have a snack break seconds prior to lunch.

"You are undoubtedly correct, Tom," I sighed. "Hungry or not, it is lunchtime. Line up and you are excused. Please walk, do not run..." And before I could blink, they were gone. Even Mrs. Duchamp had picked up her purse and was strolling out the door behind the others.

CHAPTER 12

Moping for Meatloaf

"Are you hiding?"

"Maybe."

Rob was leaning against the door frame tightly holding a cafeteria tray. "I noticed you weren't in the faculty room eating lunch," he said, watching me.

"A significant grasp of the obvious," I lamented.

"Oh, you are in a mood."

"I'm sorry. What's that hanging from your fingertips?"

"I thought you could use some nourishment since you are avoiding the teachers who are eager to speak with you."

"The hallway goes both ways, you know."

"Well, sometimes it only goes one way. Luckily, I found my way here with today's lunchtime school special."

"I'm not sure if you are being kind or trying to make me deathly ill so I would have an excuse not to give this ludicrous attempt at measuring student progress," I countered.

Rob walked over to the table I was sitting at and put the tray down. He reached for a chair and slid it next to me. As he sat down, he said, "So why are you moping?"

"Moping and mopping," I sighed as I jammed the plastic fork into what appeared to be meatloaf and pulled out the top half of the now broken fork.

Rob and I looked at each other and laughed. "Well, I tried," he said. "Now what's really got you so despondent?"

"I hate this!"

"The meatloaf? I know. Maybe it isn't meatloaf."

"It is like this ridiculous excuse of an assessment is used to destroy everything I've worked so hard to do," I said.

"Some people like meatloaf," Rob added, taking the tray and tossing the food in the garbage can. "In fact, I actually love a good meatloaf."

"For years I have tried to make an excellent meatloaf. No one would ever throw mine away because it worked, it was original, it was good, and anyone who had it would never forget it. They would grow into healthy adults and make other wonderful dishes because they never forgot how to make my meatloaf."

"Somehow I don't think you are talking about meatloaf anymore," Rob said with a quizzical expression on his face.

"Mopping and moping."

"What?"

"Why did he hate his hat? The boy will bite a bit of meatloaf,"

Rob scratched his head. "I'm starting to hate meatloaf now."

"They are pattern words from a story we have read in our reading program," I answered his query. "Rod rode his bike. He was mad his mom made him."

"Rob found his robe," Rob joined in.

We looked at each other and laughed.

Mrs. Duchamp, Jen, entered the room and also grabbed a chair. "I heard your laughter down the hallway. Mrs. Schultz was on her way down here but heard you also. She turned on her heels and fled. I wonder if she will hide or find something she hid?"

"I knew those word patterns had hidden value." I laughed harder, as did Rob and Jen.

After a short time, I stood up and grabbed some kind of beverage from the snack table. I pulled the tab and took a long drink. "Don't you get it?"

"What?" they asked in unison.

"They got it! Our kids understood the reading patterns. They were reading – really reading. Some students like Sam were doing it for the first time. And they learned it rapidly. These kids are so clever. No one gets that. This test doesn't measure that. I have been so fearful that our Resource kids would fail and feel horrible for all eternity. They will give up and never want to learn how to read because they will think that it is hopeless. But they are actually pretty smart after all."

"Are you sure it is them you are worried about or is it about you?" Rob asked gently, touching my arm.

"Maybe a little of both. I don't know honestly. But this morning was terrible. They are being horrible to each other and maybe even a bit out of control."

Mrs. Duchamp shook her head in agreement and asked rhetorically, "A bit?"

"I don't know what to do. I hate this test!" I said, putting my head on the table.

"Wait a minute," Mrs. Duchamp said sternly, standing up and crossing her arms. "I think you have lost sight of what you hold most dear."

I looked at her as if she had gone nuts. Or maybe I wondered if it was me who had lost a few brain cells.

"Might I remind you that you are a master of reinforcement and encouragement to instill motivation. You do it with fun, laughter, and a sense of accomplishment each day for each student regardless of the difficulty of the task. I've seen you work magic," my aide, friend, and coworker said directly to me. Her face turned slightly pink and there was a tremor in her fingers. I could tell she was a bit uncomfortable.

Rob continued the narrative. "Now you seem to be dissolving into a state that you have refused to let your students experience. You are better than this. Snap out of it!" I could tell that he was not uncomfortable at all.

Mrs. Duchamp wasn't done as she continued to speak with renewed determination, "And look around you. Do you know any other classroom anywhere that looks like the Old West? We can't get our kids to leave even when we want them to. Sometimes they don't want to go even if they meet eligibility criteria where they no longer qualify for Resource Room services."

My misty eyes blurred the images of my two wonderful colleagues and friends. I didn't talk. I only nodded.

Rob jumped up and swirled around. "I have to mosey on out of here and head back to the land of musical notes. Try not to step in that pile your livestock dropped on the prairie floor." And he was off.

"Speaking of musical notes, there goes that odd tingling bell telling all that lunch recess has ended. They should be here in five or ten minutes. I think I'll grab a quick cup of coffee while you gather your thoughts," she said. "Be prepared because Part II is coming!"

CHAPTER 13

Raindrops Keep Falling on My Head

I was alone in my classroom for a few moments in a whirlwind of individual activity. After a quick glance to ensure completion of a handful of important tasks, I stepped into the hallway and closed the door. I was imagining a stampede of test takers descending rapidly toward me, causing billows of dust to obscure their approach. I was wrong. My motley crew looked like drenched rats scurrying quickly while trying to escape by slip-sliding through a wet tunnel toward their intended destination.

Skidding to a collective stop directly in front of me, everyone stood frozen while water dripped into puddles around each of them.

Katie raised one hand, palm out, in a gesture similar to what I use for silence and attention. "I will be the spokesperson here!" she announced to everyone.

"What on earth?" I started to say.

"Mrs. Wright, please don't interrupt our explanation of honest and forthright facts. This is of utmost importance," Junior jumped in.

Katie raised her palm toward him and repeated, "I will be the spokesperson here!"

"OK, Katie, you have my attention," I said.

"When you excused us after our perfect and attentive morning of test taking, we went back to our classrooms in the fourth grade pod," she continued.

Junior interrupted again, "The classroom doors were locked and secured due to the strict laws regarding ridiculous and I might add mind-boggling demands for instructional protocol."

"Junior!" Katie screeched. "As I was saying, we weren't allowed in because the tests have to be protected at all costs. Our teachers had been waiting in the pod for us. They weren't happy you made us late."

Tom broke in this time. "But we told them that we were so focused on testing that we completely lost track of the time until those odd bells went off."

"TOM!" Katie screeched again. "Why can't I ever get a word in edgewise?"

I hid my expression well.

"Don't look at me like that, Mrs. Wright," Katie glared back at me. "Anyway, no more interruptions. I'm on a roll. Our teachers said that the tests had to be hidden from view because we might come in and read them."

"Obviously not realizing that we couldn't read them when we actually took the test," Sam said.

"SAM!" Katie screeched yet again. She put her fists on her hips and faced the other students. "I am the spokesperson here. Please TRY to remember that!"

"Hence the reason you, our Resource Teacher, actually reads the test to us," Tom added, grinning at Katie.

"Grrrr," Katie hissed. "So, we were told to go straight to the cafeteria for lunch."

"I did inform my teacher that I was without my necessary raingear for our upcoming recess break," Junior added.

"I was getting to that," Katie said, her irritation clear. "None of us were allowed to get our coats. So, we went to the cafeteria to eat lunch. Mrs. Schultz came in and walked to the stage microphone. She told us that it was raining outside."

"As if we weren't aware that it wasn't raining inside," Tom said.

Katie ignored him and continued, "She said we couldn't do indoor recess because the custodian had just waxed the gym floors last week and didn't want a bunch of kids destroying his work. And we couldn't go to our classrooms because of that stupid test."

"Katie," I started to admonish her but stopped abruptly.

"So, she said we all had to play in the covered play area outside. Can you imagine a few hundred of us stuffed under a weak roof in the playground basketball court area with the howling downpour threatening to drown us all? It was like sheep being forced in a controlled arena waiting to be sheared in the middle of a frigid winter!"

Almost on cue, Mrs. Duchamp appeared from around the corner holding a stack of towels. "I got these from the school nurse. I'm going to hand them out one at a time as you enter the classroom. Please try to dry off the best you can."

As everyone did as they were told, Mrs. Duchamp and I followed the students into the room. She leaned close to me and said, "Our nurse wasn't at all happy. And neither was, Doris, the secretary. I accidentally overheard an argument they were having with the principal. The secretary said she was tired of answering phone calls from parents telling her about the storm. The nurse complained about all of the students coming to her with the sniffles. There was quite a commotion in the office. I sneaked out before anyone realized I was there."

"It's always something," I said back to her. "Let's start again."

Mrs. Duchamp smiled and watched as I went over to the counter and picked up a small rectangular container. It might appear to the average person that I was holding a miniature version of a pirate's treasure chest. I always envisioned a glow would emanate from the box when the lid was opened as if it were filled with unknown sparkling diamonds, coins, and other riches. In actuality we called it Chances and it did contain treasure, but the kind of treasure that could surprise and delight any student. This box was filled with little papers folded into quarters. Each paper had something different written on it. Students could earn Chances, but they never knew what they would be getting until they pulled a paper out of the box and read it. Chances was my best and most efficient form of reinforcement. It worked miracles. I had been using Chances since the mid-1970s. The reason always remained the same, but the actual rewards evolved over time.

I stood in front of the class holding the Chances box. Everyone except our extra students, Brant and Kerry, and even Annie sat like Stepford students. Hands were folded and eyes were expectantly focused on me.

"Hey, what's going on and what is that contraption?" Brant blurted out to the group.

Katie's eyes opened wide. She turned her head toward the two boys and put a finger to her lips while raising her other hand.

"I am so pleased you remembered to raise your hand, Katie," I said. What I was actually thinking in my head was now dissolving into my own reality. It would not help to tell her what she had been doing wrong all morning. Telling her what she was doing right worked so much better. "What would you like to say?"

Katie turned toward the boys again and said, "You need to wise up."

"Katie," I jumped in, "let's try your kind words."

"So, what are you going to do, Mrs. Wright, when we don't behave?" Kerry asked. "Are you going to send us back to class or the principal?"

"Good luck with that!" Brant laughed.

Tom raised his hand. "She never does that," he said after I called on him.

I only smiled.

Annie looked around and raised her hand. "Yes, Annie," I said.

"What happened to my chair? There is a ball where my chair is supposed to be."

"That's Mrs. Wright's exercise ball, but she calls it the whirling dervish ball. I don't know why," Katie said but looked at me and put her hand over her mouth. "Sorry."

"You can sit on the ball, Annie. It will help you focus and practice staying still. But if you find your body needs to jump up and down, that is OK."

"Really?" she asked, crinkling her forehead.

"Yes."

"Kerry and I want a ball to toss around," Brant said, getting up and pushing Kerry out of his desk.

Mrs. Duchamp and I ignored him and focused on the other students. "If you will look on your desk, you will see brand new star cards."

Brant went back to his desk and picked up his 3×5 card with a baseball and mitt drawn on it. In the picture were a number of circles. "What is this?"

Tom raised his hand. I went to his desk and filled in one of the circles in his picture of a cowboy. I didn't need to say anything. Tom said to everyone, "A brief explanation is in order. When you are completing a task or doing something good, Mrs. D or Mrs. Wright will fill in a circle. We call it giving us stars on our star cards."

I responded to the curious looks on their faces. "A long time ago, they were just pieces of paper that I added stars to when students were doing well. Now we have drawings that are usually done by students."

"I have a horse," Annie said. "Can you fill in my horse? What happens when it is filled?"

Junior raised his hand. "Can I answer?"

I nodded and filled in a circle with a star on his card, which had a picture of stylish western boots.

"We proceed to the store, and we can either save the Resource money we earn by putting it in our individual banks or spend it. Each star or point, as they sometimes describe it, is worth one cent. You need a whole $3.00 to buy Chances. But that is the greatest thing ever!"

A chorus of "YES" filled the air, but I let that go.

Kerry was starting to comprehend. He raised his hand, and I nodded while walking over and putting a star on his basketball picture. "Can we go to the store, too? And can we get Chances? What is so wonderful about Chances anyway?"

Everyone had their hands up. I called on them one at a time so they could describe the Chances they had gotten throughout the year.

"I got a new pencil. It was the Herman H. Hilfinker the III, Junior, special edition. I am still not sure how that happened," Junior said.

"I got to sit in my chair backwards all day!"

"Remember when we all got to go for an extra recess because of me?"

"I got to give another Chance to anyone of my choice."

"I got a get-out-of-homework-free card."

"Mine was better. I got a get-out-of-trouble-free card. I'm still saving that one.

"Oh, and remember a few months ago, Katie got the grand prize!"

Katie beamed from ear to ear. "We all got to watch a movie and eat popcorn all because of me!"

I interrupted everyone by putting my hand up with my palm forward. "One, two, three. Eyes on me." Katie closed her mouth and looked at me with her eyes wide open. "This afternoon we are going to start over. All our classroom rules and expectations will be in place as will our prizes and rewards. And as a special bonus, Chances is waiting for one person to pick out a surprise that will be given to everyone in the room!"

Cheers and clapping erupted. Mrs. Duchamp mouthed, "You're magic!"

As we smiled at the captive audience we were facing, immediate silence ensued, and they became the Stepford students again. The rain had stopped abruptly. A stillness wrapped around the room as an ominous glow filtered through the windows. A chill seemed to seep into everyone as we all were shivering. I turned around to see what they were staring at. Mrs. Schultz was in the doorway.

CHAPTER 14

The Time The Lights Went Out

"I wasn't going to disturb you, but I see it wouldn't matter anyway. You should have started testing when recess ended twenty-one minutes ago," Mrs. Schultz said wringing her hands, then gesturing me toward her. "May I have a word?" She stopped for a breath and finally said, "Please!"

Mrs. Shultz was a solid woman shaped like a box with arms sticking out of each side and a round head floating on top. Her hair was a mixture of gray and black reminiscent of an overprocessed perm from days gone by. I always thought her face could be somewhat pretty if only she were able to remove that permanent scowl. At that moment, the scowl deepened, causing excessive creases. I took a deep breath and walked slowly toward her. My classroom continued to be eerily still and quiet. I think everyone wanted to eavesdrop. That really would be unnecessary since Mrs. Schultz has a booming voice that tends to reverberate off the walls wherever she goes, even when she is deliberately trying to whisper.

"Someone stole towels from the office. Do you know anything about that?" she asked.

"Towels?" I asked as if I had never heard the word before.

From around the corner, Mrs. Duchamp materialized holding a large stack of wet towels. She looked at us as if she had no idea what was going on. "Oh, Mrs. Schultz, it was so kind of you to be concerned for our students in their time of need. They followed the expectations of outdoor rainy day recess, but that storm managed to attack each and every one of them with a deluge of rain that soaked into their clothes. You were so considerate to have these towels ready and waiting for them. I have always admired how you are right on top of these things."

I turned and gave Mrs. Duchamp a look that said, You are laying it on a bit thick don't you think? But since I'm very good at keeping my expressions hidden, she didn't react. She only smiled, dropped the towels into Mrs. Schultz's arms, and walked back into the classroom.

The soggy towels fell almost immediately to the floor. Mrs. Schultz put her head back into the classroom and said, "I could use some help carrying these to the office." No response. "Please."

As if we were in a B movie, a crack of thunder split the sound barrier. The girls screamed and the boys froze. Simultaneously every student flew their hand straight and high in the air while saying, "I'll help, Mrs. Schultz!" Then without warning, the lights went out, leaving us in darkness.

Mrs. Schultz spun around and headed back down the hallway toward the office. "If it is not one thing, it is another," we heard her bellow. "I have to deal with one crisis here and another one over there. It never ends, I tell you. I am always dealing with something and does anyone give ME credit? NO! One complaint after another."

I watched from my doorway as I saw Mr. Dustler, the custodian, turn the corner toward the principal. He tried to reverse and turn back, but it was too late. "Mr. Dustler," Mrs. Schultz screeched, "Stop right there in your tracks. Do not move an inch!"

"Yes, Mrs. Schultz. Do you want something?"

"The lights are out!" she yelled at him.

"Really?" he said facetiously.

The principal's face turned bright red, and her scowl deepened with every angry word said pointedly one at a time. "How. Did. It. Happen?"

"How would I know?" he yelled back. "Do you think I am in constant communication with the electric company? Or possibly I get messages from the beyond."

"Hardly, who'd want to talk to you? Just get it fixed. NOW! It started in the Resource Room." She started to walk into the office, but before going in, she turned around and said, "Please."

"How would those little monsters know how to turn off the lights? I wouldn't put it past them, though," he mumbled as he quickly approached and followed me into the classroom.

Mr. Dustler stood stock still at the entrance. He was extremely pale, thin as a rail, and so tall that his head almost hit the top of the doorframe. He cast a flashlight's beam around the room, exposing each frightened child one by one. He returned the beam to just under his face, causing a ghostly apparition. The girls and maybe a few boys screamed again.

"You don't have any lights," Mr. Dustler said.

"Really?" Brant said sarcastically.

I gave Brant the famous teacher look but doubted he could have seen it or even if it would have made any difference. So, I directed my response toward the custodian. "Do you know what happened, and can you fix it?"

"Do I look like an electrician to you? I am not exactly on their first call list. Or maybe you think a higher power is in personal touch with me?" he grumbled to nobody.

"Not likely. I thought it might be the storm," I said.

"Anything is possible," he answered back.

Mrs. Duchamp again appeared out of nowhere. "I was wondering if you knew how to fix it. You are so clever with mechanics or whatever it is that needs to be done. We are so lucky to have you here in our time of need."

I turned and gave her my nondescript look again. She only smiled.

"I will do my utmost to see what is going on for you, Mrs. Duchamp." He leaned over and whispered to her, "But not for her."

Brant got tired of swinging his arm back and forth. He finally got up and said to the custodian, "The school has a generator, you know. The generator is for emergencies like this. It will give us power."

"I know that, you little scamp. How do you know about the generator?" Mr. Dustler asked.

"I saw it in the back of your custodian closet, which is really more like a conference room filled with janitor stuff."

"You are not allowed in my area. What were you doing there? I keep it locked!"

"Just doing a little exploring and I must have gotten lost. I heard the principal stomping down the hall, so with a few bobby pins and my ingenuity, it just popped open."

Mr. Dustler stared at Brant and hissed, "I am going to tell the principal what you've been up to."

Brant only shrugged his shoulders and said, "Did I mention that it smelled like smoke in there?"

Our custodian made a swift turn, causing him to slip on the damp floor and wet towels. He grabbed the coatrack, and everything came tumbling down on top of him. I gasped and went to try to help him up. He pushed me away angrily. "Get this cleaned up. Where's your mop? Why are there wet towels here? There should be a school law," he shouted.

"You have the mops, Mr. Dustler," I said. "We would appreciate it if you would kindly take care of this."

"I have to get the power on. Those towels and this mess are not in my job description. That is teacher work," he said glowering.

"We can send a student to help get the mop," Mrs. Duchamp said. "While you are doing that out of the generosity of your soul, I will gather a number of sweatshirts and jackets from the Lost and Found that we might borrow for today." She looked back over at me and continued, "At the same time, I will get the key for the locked cabinet where the emergency supplies are kept."

"Good idea, Mrs. Duchamp. I am glad someone around here is capable of handling the situation. "Just don't send that menace over there," he said, pointing directly at Brant.

Kerry jumped up and raced to pick up the towels. "I'll do it, Mrs. Wright and Mrs. Duchamp. You don't need to worry about a thing. I am Brant's accomplice after all, so I know what I'm doing!"

He sprinted out of the room before either of us could respond.

CHAPTER 15

Your Silhouette Is Showing

The rain returned with a vengeance. Although it was still dark, it didn't seem as pitch black as it was earlier when the thunder terrified us all. Now I could make out a few shapes and could certainly hear sounds, including the incessant irritable moans and complaining from everyone, me included. My irritation stayed in my head of course, and no one was able to read my thoughts or decipher my expressions this time.

"So, boys and girls, I don't believe we can continue testing at the moment. Let's wait until Mrs. Duchamp returns with the key to unlock the cabinet that contains the emergency kit. Then we should have plenty of flashlights to help us. In the meantime, let's take a short break. Please stay in your seats, however, because you may stumble into someone or something if you move around." An array of cheers or maybe groans filled the atmosphere, so I added, "You can talk freely amongst yourselves as long as you are quiet and kind."

I noticed that Laine's hand had been flying back and forth. I pointed to him and nodded that I was aware he had something to say. As if a thinking bubble popped in my head, I said, "Oh, Laine, I'm so sorry. I wasn't cognizant..."

"What is that supposed to mean?" Katie interrupted.

"It means she didn't realize," Sam cut in.

"Yes, thank you, Sam. You are right in more ways than one," I answered.

"Mrs. Wright," Katie said, "I don't think Laine can see you. That might be why he has large print."

"Or it may be because it is dark in here," I responded.

"I can see in the dark just fine. I'm used to it," Laine said. "These gigantic papers are my mom's idea." He put his hand down and laid his head on his desk.

Not afraid to get his two cents in, Tom said, "Mrs. Wright, when you make a mistake, you give us a star on our star cards. And since we are doing Math for the entire day..."

"Which is unconscionable, I might add," Sam broke in again.

Katie hissed but somehow managed to keep her comments to herself.

"As I was saying," Tom said, "I am now counting at least two mistakes, but there will undoubtedly be more."

"Indubitably," Sam added.

Although I couldn't see her face, I was pretty sure Katie was crossing her eyes. "You are absolutely correct. I am adding two points or stars to everyone's star card," I said.

I walked around giving the points and ended up at Laine's desk. I knelt down next to his chair and spoke quietly to him alone. "Laine, I want to tell you how impressed I have been today watching you. Your wonderful attitude and determination should be a lesson to us all. I am sorry I didn't respond verbally to your raised hand. I wasn't thinking and I made a mistake."

"I'm not upset with you, Mrs. Wright. I make mistakes all the time, but I try to hide them. You let everyone see yours. Is that better?"

"I don't know, Laine."

Since I was fairly close to Laine, I could see that his face showed clear consternation. He seemed to be struggling with his thoughts. After a minute of silence, he looked directly at me with damp eyes and said, "I don't know either, but maybe it is good to do both."

As I struggled back to a standing position, Sam hollered, "I think I see Mrs. Duchamp's silhouette in the doorway."

Katie clearly had had enough. She hissed at Sam, "Why do you always say those big words that no one understands, not even you?"

"I understand them. It is not my fault that you don't."

"I know what silly wet whatever means," she countered.

"No, you don't."

"Yes, I do," Katie yelled. "Mrs. Wright, Sam is doing it again! He is acting like a teacher!"

Passing by their desks and heading toward Mrs. Duchamp, I said, "Maybe he is practicing for the future."

I overheard Sam mumble under his breath, "Maybe I am."

"So how is this behavior modification working out for you?" Mrs. Duchamp asked in an uncharacteristic manner while handing me the clothing.

"It works better in the light of day and when I'm not so frazzled."

"I can see that. Well, I can't actually see much of anything, but here are the keys."

"Keys?" I questioned, taking a huge ring of keys from her and handing the jackets to Sam to pass out. "We need one key."

"I know. Unfortunately, I tried to explain that to our lovely school secretary, but I'm afraid I got an earful. I escaped mid tirade."

"Why aren't these labeled?"

"Do you really want to hear her answer to that very reasonable question?"

"It boggles the mind. Oh well. Would you kindly start with one and try to open the cabinet?"

"So, take your pick. Which key should I try first?" Mrs. Duchamp asked, jangling the huge mass of keys in her hands.

Every hand went up. I didn't think they were spying on us, but I should have known better. "OK, let's see who is sitting quietly."

The Stepford students were at their peak of attentiveness. I walked around the desks deliberately as if I was a game show host. "I think I will choose Laine," I announced. The class erupted in applause and cheers. I was astonished. They always do something that surprises me.

Laine held the bundle of keys, which seemed twice as large in his small hands. He raised the items to within an inch of his eyes and rifled through them. "This is the lucky key," he said, handing the one key out over the others.

"Here you go, Mrs. Duchamp. Try this one first and then proceed with the rest," I said as she took the keys from me and went over to the cabinet.

"This will undoubtedly take a while," I said.

"Indubitably," Sam said, grinning while giving each student either a jacket or a sweatshirt to put on over their damp clothes.

"Stop! I can't stand it," Katie hollered back.

"And they're back," I must have said out loud.

"And so am I," Mrs. Duchamp said.

"What?"

"The first key worked."

"Will wonders never cease?" I said, surprised.

Mrs. Duchamp pulled out a large container clearly marked "Emergency Kit." We opened it up together and rummaged through the various items meant for whatever emergency should come our way. "Where are the flashlights?" I asked.

After digging a bit deeper to the bottom of the container, she pulled out the one and only flashlight. "Well, better than nothing, I suppose," I said, trying to flick it on and off, but no light emanated from it.

"Let me see," she said. After opening the flashlight up and looking inside, she closed it back up again and said, "There are no batteries."

With every facetious thought in my head, I said to no one and everyone, "Oh how I wish I was Samantha from *Bewitched* right now and could twitch my nose, twirl my arms around, and chant, "Lights obey, do what I say, turn yourself on so we can be done today!"

The lights miraculously flickered back on. A few individuals gasped. Or maybe that was me.

Brant looked befuddled and said, "How did you do that?"

Annie spoke in almost a frightened whisper, “Maybe she is a wizard?”

“Magic,” Mrs. Duchamp said to me with a wink.

CHAPTER 16

Can I Have a Proctor, Please?

Kerry strutted into the classroom like a peacock full of his self-appointed and somewhat arrogant pride. "I saved the day, everyone. Have no fear, Kerry is here!"

Even I groaned this time and said, "Yes, the power is back on. Or I have the power. The jury is still out on that. We don't know for how long, so please return to your desk so we can commence our testing once again and this time hopefully without interruptions."

Kerry ignored me and said to the class at large, "I showed Mr. Dustler how to turn the generator on. I know how because we have one at home. My dad taught me. I think I might have to be an engineer someday to save the world from people who don't know how to use a generator."

"Please open your test booklets. There is a paper insert where you left off." Mrs. Duchamp and I put stars on the star cards and gave positive reinforcement to those following directions. Kerry and Brant looked confused but gave each other what might have been a secret sign and actually did what the others were doing. When I saw that they had complied and were now ready to start working, I strolled over and put points down, nodding with my own secret sign as I did so.

"Everyone, I want to remind you to write your name on the upper right hand corner of each piece of scrap paper," I said, almost cringing before asking the next question. "Now, are there any questions before you begin?"

Tom's hand flew into the air. "Mrs. Wright, Mrs. Wright, does that mean that if my name is Tom, I write Tom on the paper?"

Instead of answering, I stole a look at the clock and turned my attention to Mrs. Duchamp. "Don't forget that you have afternoon recess duty in fifteen minutes."

"No, I convinced Mrs. Schultz that she was correct in assuming I would be needed here for testing today. So, she almost kindly agreed that she would cover for me."

The intercom screeched on, almost deafening us. Someone was blowing into the microphone on their end. "Hello, hello. Can you hear me? Is this on? Oh, OK then. Hello, students, this is your principal, Mrs. Schultz, speaking. I have an important announcement to make. There will be no outdoor recess this afternoon. Your teachers can decide if they want you to have one in your classrooms. That is all." The intercom went silent. Everyone sighed.

"I'll take the clever pups section, if you would handle the smart cats for now," I said to Mrs. Duchamp, who I could tell felt a bit guilty but tried not to show it.

She nodded and instructed her group of five to begin. I gathered my four and started again. "The next question is multiple choice. I will read the question and the three possible answers." After I did so, I monitored the students. Sam hovered his pencil over a possible answer A and glared up at me. I gave him no response. He moved his pencil again and circled it above possible answer B. He squinted his eyes tighter at me. I gave no response. He went to possible answer C and stared without blinking like a cat ready to pounce at its prey. The odd thought in my head was that I misnamed the instructional areas. They should have been called the cats instead of dogs. I did not budge, but instead said, "Are you ready to go to the next one?"

Shane shouted from across the room, "That's a question, isn't it? I need to go back to that problem when I was asked to write a question. I know what a question is now. Mrs. D, help me find that old question? That's a question, too, isn't it? I know all sorts of questions now!"

Mrs. Duchamp handled the situation like the pro she was, and I ignored Shane and shifted my attention back to Sam. "Mrs. Wright, would you please just look at me?" asked Sam.

"Just fill in the circle," I said dramatically.

Sam looked at me coyly and tried again, "Let me just look at your face as I point to each multiple choice answer with my number two pencil."

"Just please take a good guess and go on," I pleaded.

"No," he exclaimed, "I have to get it right! It's going to traumatize me for the rest of my life!"

I gently touched Sam on the back and in a quiet and soothing voice told him not to give up because there were many items he might not know. He answered back, "You have got to be kidding! How the tarnation am I supposed to know this? I am in the Resource Room. Hasn't anyone figured that out yet?"

Tom, who had been observing Annie earlier, and was now taking the test in every possible position except actually sitting on his chair, said in a very high-strung voice, "I believe this is just a political maneuver by Clinton to..."

I interrupted, "Can we just do the problems and not have a political discussion?"

"My turn," Mrs. Duchamp said, exchanging places with me.

I walked over and sat between Shane and Junior. The next problem showed a picture of some pigs and asked to give an estimate of the sum total of 29 pigs and 19 pigs. Shane counted each pig with his pencil eraser tip, then realized that the actual number of pigs and the numbers given in the four multiple-choice options were not the same. Shane's anxiety hit a new high. He fidgeted and got extremely agitated. He grabbed his ruler and spun it around. He kept repeating, "Stupid pigs, stupid pigs." I kept trying to encourage him to simply give it his best guess and move on, but there was no consoling him. Just as I was tempted to fill in the darn circle myself, he jumped up and exclaimed, "This is going to make me into a druggie!" He grabbed his pencil in his fist and rammed it down on the desk. I seized his test in the nick of time.

Shane exploded, shouting, "My pencil is broken!"

Test taking came to a complete stop. Mrs. Duchamp and I stared at each other in horror.

"Use the other one, Shane," I said.

"No! I have to use this one. My teacher gave this one to me. She said it was my lucky pencil. If I don't use this one, I won't be lucky. I'll forget everything. My brain will stop working."

Katie added to the chaos without raising her hand. "He'll flunk, Mrs. Wright, and it'll be your fault. Maybe he should go tell the principal."

I stepped in front of Shane before he tried to flee out the door. Mrs. Duchamp put her back to Katie and quietly reinforced the other students, who were not getting involved in this particular drama. As she added points for them and not Katie, she turned back around and noticed that Katie had started working again.

"Let's sharpen your lucky pencil," I said to Shane without paying any attention to Katie or the others.

Mrs. Duchamp turned her head toward me with panic in her eyes. "The pencil sharpener is broken. A few weeks ago, you requisitioned a new one, but were told you would have to buy that out of your own pocket."

"I remember," I said, frustrated, and returned to focus on how to help Shane.

Surprisingly, Junior came to our assistance. "I have my very own Herman H. Hilfinker the III, Junior, pencil sharpener," he said. "But only I can use it."

"Junior, we would be very grateful if you would kindly sharpen Shane's pencil," I said.

"Well, I will if the garbage can sit next to me the whole time just in case Jimmy comes over here and throws up. I don't want throw-up on my test."

"Deal!"

A quick exchange was made, and Shane returned to his test completely oblivious to the previous commotion. I went back over to the pup section.

"Tom, are you sleeping?" I asked as I sat down next to him.

"No." Tom had two pencils and a bookmark encircling a word on his test. His eyes were about two inches from the booklet. One eye was closed.

"What are you doing?" I inquired.

"I'm trying to look at one word at a time."

"Oh."

"If I look at too many letters at a time, I get dizzy," he said.

At the same time, Jimmy stretched his arms up to the ceiling and froze.

After encouraging Tom to do his best, I asked Jimmy if he needed some help, although I knew I couldn't really do much in the way of assistance.

"I can't write," Tom said.

"Why not?" I replied.

"My legs are bugging me."

"Then I think it would be a good idea to just use your hands to write."

Even with the rain drumming a cacophony of beats against the windowpane, I could hear Brant whispering to Mrs. Duchamp. "Are you like a proctor?" he asked her.

"What do you mean?" she asked.

"In my class we have a proctor. My teacher said this proctor man was probably for me," he said.

"Is that like proctor and gambles?" Annie broke in.

"I didn't know we could gamble in the Resource Room. I was wondering why there were dice in the box," Kerry said.

"Cool," came the unified response.

"Now I really want to come here," said Brant and Kerry almost simultaneously.

CHAPTER 17

Are We Done Yet?

Within the next hour, one by one, each student was done. I gave a sigh of relief and said, "You did it! I am so proud of every one of you. Go ahead and get up. Feel free to stretch your fatigued muscles and visit the snack table before heading back to class."

"That's a good one," Sam said. "I better jot 'fatigued muscles' down in my compilation dictionary of odd Mrs. Wright sayings."

I looked at him sideways without making a comment. "Test one, Math Estimation, is completed!" A cheer went up.

"Not a moment too soon," Tom said as he munched on a couple of cookies and headed back to his desk.

"Mrs. Wright," Katie wailed, "typically we get out of school around this time."

"Yes," several of the other students, who were mingling around the snack table, agreed.

Mrs. Duchamp nodded a few times and corralled the remaining students back to their desks. She pointed to the clock while clearing her throat.

"You have to do Chances first," Katie said in a loud voice so no one could ignore her, including me.

"Thank you for reminding me, Katie," I said.

"No problem, Mrs. Wright. And I won't forget about researching senior colonies for you, too."

"Yes, well, I am looking for someone that will choose the Chance for everyone here. Even though we had a few mishaps, I still believe Chances are in order," I said.

Everyone sat quietly at their desk with hands folded and eyes looking at the shiny box filled with surprises. The excitement mounted as I looked around to pick someone I thought did the best that they could. "This is a difficult choice as you all tried and worked hard during a difficult situation. But for today, Junior, come on down!"

The class cheered for Junior, which made him grin from ear to ear. He stood up and walked to the front of the room with deliberation and purpose. "I want to thank you all for acknowledging the importance of this moment. I will now commence to choose the best and most relevant Chance."

I opened the lid as everyone held their breath. Junior pulled out a square piece of paper and handed it to me. I handed it back to him and said, "You can unfold it and read it to the class."

He smiled broadly and did as he was instructed. After reading it to himself, his smiling face turned from a happy glow to a confused grimace. "You get a brand new number two pencil!"

"Just in time for tomorrow's testing. That is wonderful!" I said, trying to be excited.

No one said a word, but I knew what they were thinking. "Well, it is a Chance," I continued. "You get what you get, and you don't throw a fit."

"That's OK, Mrs. Wright," Katie said, turning to face the others. "You never know what you'll get in here. Sometimes it's exciting and sometimes it's a bore. You never know."

"Ten more minutes and the buses will be here to take you home," I said. "Please leave your test booklets on your desk with the jackets or sweatshirts from lost and found."

As the students were getting ready to leave, Tom asked, "What test do we have to do tomorrow?"

"Tomorrow, we will take the Reading Comprehension WASL," I replied.

"We?" Tom questioned with a serious tone in his voice. "Does that mean YOU have to take it, too?"

"Well, no, but..."

"Why is the WASL given anyway?" Tom asked.

I thought about it for a moment before responding, "Well, one of the reasons is to help the teachers know how they are doing."

Tom didn't miss a beat. "Then let the teachers take it!"

Always eager to get into the act, Katie followed Tom's response with her own comment. "Do you know something, Mrs. Wright?" she asked.

I shrugged my shoulders, so she continued. "Do you know how confusing this WASL is? It is harder than figuring out what a boy is thinking!" She took off her assigned jacket and turned to walk away.

Mrs. Duchamp came over and looked at me thoughtfully before saying, "You know something, I think she is right."

"Thanks, boys and girls, you can go back to class and get your things before heading out to the buses. Please remember that tomorrow..." but no one was paying attention to me.

All eyes were turned toward Shane. Jimmy jumped up. Annie fell off the big round whirling dervish ball that had worked so well all afternoon. Katie's eyes were wide open, yet her mouth stayed tightly closed.

"You need to do something, Mrs. Wright," came the frantic cries from all around us.

CHAPTER 18

No Tests Were Harmed

A number of students screeched and tried to out-holler each other, "Look at Shane!" Mrs. Duchamp and I turned as one toward Shane. His hands were firmly over his mouth and his face was beet red. Time passed in tedious slow motion. I remember somehow knocking over someone's chair, vaulting over Sam's desk, and flying toward Shane. My two arms were outstretched like a middle-aged Supergirl to the rescue. My fingertips reached their target and the test booklet slid off Shane's desk and somersaulted into the air. Mrs. Duchamp instinctively sailed toward the target more competently than any receiver at the goalpost in the final seconds of a championship Super Bowl football game. Cheers erupted from the sidelines at the exact moment when the Mt. Shane volcano exploded in tiny snack-like chunks down my hair and clothes.

Junior had jumped back during the ordeal and now tilted his head toward Shane and me. "Hmmm," he said shrugging his shoulders, "I thought it would be Jimmy. Well, that was an error in judgment." He quickly retrieved a Herman Hilfinker the III, Junior, monogrammed handkerchief out of his inside jacket pocket and put it over his nose and mouth.

"I certainly hope that test will not have to go into one of those highly irregular special plastic bags which must be sent to a toxic disposal facility before it can be scored," a familiar voice said. "Do you have any idea how many procedural forms you would have to fill out in triplicate?"

"Thank you, Mrs. Schultz," I managed to say, disentangling myself from the slippery surface of Shane's desk. "We have this under control. No test was harmed in this unusual situation."

The principal continued to linger by the doorway. "Children, Mrs. Wright must have forgotten to dismiss you. It is time to go home."

"She didn't forget, Mrs. Schultz," Katie began; "she was preoccupied."

I smiled at Katie and softly suggested that everyone return to their own classrooms to be dismissed. The children chatted amicably as they exited the classroom. Jimmy, however, strolled up to me and tugged on my wet sleeve. "You kind of smell funny, Mrs. Wright."

"My dog would notice right away. Hey, Jimmy, do you think you have a dog smelling nose?" Tommy added as they both ambled out of the room.

"I'll go ask Mr. Holden, our favorite music teacher, if he has an outfit you could borrow from his theatrical costume room," Mrs. Duchamp said.

"You will do no such thing. It is almost three o'clock. Your contractual employment time is over, and you should go home," I said without conviction.

"I'm not sure that is wise," she began but wasn't allowed to finish.

"Nope, that was our agreement. No overtime," I said. "I'm not sure whose idiotic idea that was, but it is what we decided,"

"That's what you decided," she said. "You got it into your head that I don't get paid enough, which I actually agree with. But that doesn't mean I shouldn't work past 3:00."

"They don't pay you overtime, remember?"

"I am needed here right now, so...," she started again but I interrupted her.

"Nope, off you go."

"Are you forgetting that you go beyond your expected hours day after day and probably weekends, too?"

"I can do it," Sam said, turning his head back and forth between us. We hadn't even realized that he was still there.

"Good idea, Sam," Mrs. Duchamp said as she was getting her purse out of the closet and putting on her jacket. "Tell Mr. Holden that this situation is urgent. He will understand."

Sam took off like a speeding bullet.

"Go home and relax," I said to Mrs. Duchamp. "Try to get ready for tomorrow's Reading Comprehension assessment."

Mrs. Duchamp headed toward the door and turned back toward me. "Don't look so forlorn. Only five more days of testing, then we can start the Science Fair projects," she pointed out, smirking.

"Yikes, don't remind me. I'm stressed enough. Go, goodbye already."

"Jimmy is right, you do reek. This Old West is more authentic now. It smells like a pig farm." She left, chuckling.

I yelled after her, "Don't remind me of pigs, either!"

As I headed toward the sink to try to wash some of the regurgitated snack bar off me, Sammy careened around the corner and into the room. "Mrs. Schultz is on my tail. Here you go, Mrs. Wright," he said tossing a large bag at me and turning around. He somehow managed to reduce his speed to a slow crawl, anticipating the principal's arrival.

I raced in front of him to the doorway and caught a glimpse of Mrs. Schultz waving her arms. "Run, Sammy," I urged in a heightened whisper.

"You always tell me not to run down the hallway," he countered, slowing his pace even more defiantly.

Now he listened to me. It never stopped him before, I said silently to myself.

"SAMMY!" Mrs. Schultz's shrieking was getting closer. "The buses are waiting for you! Hurry up!"

"I am following the long-established and honored rule of 'no running in the halls,'" Sammy said, tiptoeing deliberately out the door.

"You can disobey that directive this once. "You have my permission," the principal almost begged.

"Oh, no, I would not want to lose your respect for not following the rules, but if you would like to address that in writing, I would consider it."

I peered around the doorway and watched as Sammy sauntered toward the entrance at the front of the school. Mrs. Schultz huffed and swiftly turned on her heels and headed back toward the Resource Room. I quickly ducked into the room and headed toward the sink.

"I should hope you are looking under that cabinet for cleaning supplies," she wailed when entering the room.

"Can Mr. Dustler, our custodian, clean this up?" I asked. "He has all the necessary supplies."

Mrs. Schultz creased her already wrinkled brow. "Well, since you asked, I will tell you. I ordered him to guard the locked conference room where I am storing tomorrow's Reading Comprehension test booklets. He had the audacity to inform me that he had left his six-shooter at home and needed to go retrieve it."

It would have been so easy to burst into laughter, but instead I only said, "Whatever did he mean by that?"

"I have no idea. Please clean this up," she said, leaving the classroom. She poked her head back around and added, "And yourself, too. You smell terrible."

Masking my inner merriment, I enjoyed the fact that our otherwise annoying Mr. Dustler put one over on our astute principal. Our fearless custodian lived across the sound. The ferry ride took at least forty minutes one way to get to the other side. I chuckled as I stood alone in my Resource Room.

Uniquely Us – Tales from a Resource Room

CHAPTER 19

This Outfit Seems Appropriate

The welcoming quiet was mesmerizing, but the smell was nauseating. I picked up the bag and took a quick glance inside. After rummaging through the entire contents, the only thing I could do was moan internally. The women's restroom was in the corner of the staff room. That is where I needed to go immediately. As I walked down a deserted hallway, I chanted a silent mantra, Please don't let anyone be in there, please don't let anyone be in there.

"Look what the cat dragged in," Mr. Sonic, the PE teacher, exclaimed as I peeked into the faculty lounge.

"Cat? Try farm animals!" one of the other teachers laughingly replied, causing the full house to make horrible guffawing noises. There must have been at least a couple dozen jovial staff members observing me.

"I have never seen this room stuffed with so many people. How did you manage it?" I questioned.

"We heard through the grapevine that you encountered some typical difficulties today and we knew it would only be a matter of time until you made your way here," Mrs. Wilson, a fourth grade teacher, said.

"Besides, after the testing day we've had, it seemed a little levity was warranted," another of my fourth grade comrades added.

"A testing mishap," I began. No one was listening to me. Most were making odd jokes or snickering as I was dripping in the middle of the room. A dozen or so teachers swiftly fled when the stench became obvious.

The intern for our school counselor tried to display compassion. She walked up to me, put her hand on my shoulder and immediately took two paces backwards. Looking forlorn, she said, "I believe it may be possible for me to open my calendar and find a fifteen-minute appointment time for you."

"Whatever for?" I asked the young lady, who couldn't be much older than twenty-two.

"This would be a time to connect with your inner self. A time to get in touch with your emotionally despondent true spirit. Maybe I should check for a thirty-minute slot?"

"Thank you, but no thanks. I just need to go clean up now," I told her with an urgency to get into the restroom behind her.

"I believe this is open for therapeutic debate. There is a strong possibility that I could bring this unique case up for discussion in my Abnormal Psychology class," the counseling intern said.

I ignored her and found my attention pulled in another direction. "Speaking of psychs," I said sharply, noticing our school psychologist trying to sneak out the back door.

I rushed toward the exit to confront her. "Hang on, Mrs. Beetle. When are you going to finish the cognitive assessments on our referrals? We have four children on the testing schedule. I finished the academic portion weeks ago. The clock is running out."

"You can't expect me to rush these things," she said, opening the door.

"Wait," I said a little too loudly.

Mrs. Wilson was sitting at a table by the exit door. She turned her attention to our discussion. "One of those referrals is a student of mine. I talked to the parents the other day. I had to make excuses why this was taking so long."

"Why is it taking so long?" I asked.

"I can't very well conduct cognitive testing when you are all doing the WASL. That would totally confuse those little children," Mrs. Beetle said.

"So, what are you doing instead?" Mrs. Wilson asked.

"I am assessing and contemplating what should occur next in the process," she said.

"I've got an idea," I said. "You could help give the standardized WASL testing."

"I must apologize, but clearly you can see that providing you with assistance would unnecessarily compete with both my professional demeanor and my ability to provide appropriate psychological evaluations," she said and rushed out the door.

As if anyone would be able to tell, I said under my breath, but I was pretty sure Mrs. Wilson read my thoughts.

I meandered my way back toward the ladies room. The intern quickly got out of my way and out of my visual range. Once inside, I washed up as best as I could and changed into Rob's unique and equally annoying apparel selection. I put my head under the cold-water faucet since there was no hot water. At the same time, I continually pushed the lever on the soap dispenser. I am not sure why I was surprised that it was empty. With eyes closed and my head still under the running water, I reached toward the square paper towel unit on the wall trying to feel for the little crooked handle so I could crank it around, allowing the dingy brown, scratchy paper towels to roll out. Nothing. There were no towels. Again, why was I surprised? I lifted my head and felt a quick pain on the back of my head from the faucet. Growling, I put on the outfit and headed back out the door.

The faculty lounge exploded into laughter. I felt myself turn beet red and rushed out the door as fast as a racehorse, heading toward the Resource Room before anyone else could make a snide remark.

Sitting on one of the student desks was Rob Holden, the music teacher. Our wonderful friendship was at that moment teetering on the edge of my endurance. I relaxed, though, when I saw him. Rob was my favorite colleague and closest confidant. I really did enjoy his mischievous nature. He reminded me a little of a cross between Beethoven and John Lennon. He was musically brilliant and cynically devious, and I loved it.

"Saddle up to the bar and I'll buy you a drink," Rob said, handing me a bottle of Diet Dr. Pepper.

Without acknowledgment I took a quick swig and sighed, "So horribly warm. Another surprise. Did I ever tell you what I said to my last principal before I left for another district?" Without waiting for an answer, I continued, "I am leaving because there is no Diet Dr. Pepper in the pop machine."

"Only a couple hundred times, Rosie," he answered with a grin.

"A couple hundred? You are keeping track?"

"Of course. I have a jar that I put a marble in every time I hear that remembrance," he said. "I am going to have to get a bigger jar."

"Why this outfit? Are you crazy?" I glared at him.

"Well, I thought about Miss Beadle or Miss Kitty, but this seemed more fitting."

"Annie Oakley?" I smirked.

"I am thinking about doing *Annie Get Your Gun*."

"This is an elementary school, you fool," I said, turning toward the snack table and picking up a glazed pastry. "Wait, hang on. I know. I will rewrite the musical for you so it can be age appropriate and politically astute." I swiveled back toward him and swept my donut held hand high into the open air in front of me, imagining the Broadway marquee. "*Annie Get Your Donut*!!"

"Hello. Excuse me," a soft unknown voice came from the doorway.

CHAPTER 20

This Might Look a Little Strange

A perfectly proportioned, slender, and elegantly dressed woman interrupted our bantering. She wore a silk blouse with a large sash that was tied in a bow at her neck. A vest with pearl buttons fitted snugly over the blouse. It matched the pencil skirt that stopped slightly below her knees. Black, shiny high heels added to the complete fashion statement. But what struck me the most was the hat that sat tilted on a professionally styled Vidal Sassoon bobbed haircut. She was movie star elegant walking into a theatrical set. This woman reminded me of my mother's closest friend, Veronica, in their younger days when I was a child. I liked her instantly.

"I love your hat" was all I could say.

"Thank you. I made it," she answered as she looked curiously around the room and surreptitiously at me.

Rob broke through my contemplation. "Well, looks like I should mosey on out of here."

"So, go ahead and head into the sunset on your fawn-colored mule," I called after him.

"Try not to step into anything," he countered and left.

I laughed but stopped suddenly when I realized what this woman must be thinking. My hair was still dripping on my cowgirl western shirt. An enormous silver buckle was attached to the belt that tugged at the oversized rawhide pants with little cut-outs. The donut was crushed in my hand, which I immediately hid behind my back. At least I was cognizant enough to drop the donut onto the table behind me. What I did not realize was that I was standing in the residual lava disaster.

Her head was tilted, and her eyes surveyed everything around her. "I can see why now," she only said.

"Oh," I said, not understanding who she was or why she was there. I only wanted to escape but felt trapped. I was envisioning what it would be like to have one of those giant water containers that animals used to drink from out on the farm and to be able to soak in it endlessly. The crazy thoughts must have made me fidget or maybe I was audibly sighing. I was jolted to consciousness when I finally noticed her watching me.

"I am Mrs. Margaret Harrigan. My daughter is Annie Harrigan. She came home today insisting that we change our last name to Oakley and that she should have a horse. She claimed that only then would she be able to be a Resource student and go to your class every day."

"Oh?"

"I was not even aware she started coming for lessons in here. Isn't this a Special Education classroom? It is not how I envisioned a Special Education program would look like. Should I not have been notified at least? I was under the impression I would need to give my consent."

"I am sorry about the confusion and the current state of things here," I said. "It is a little more difficult than getting a name change or a horse."

"Not to me it isn't."

"I wonder why Annie would think those were the criteria?" I questioned out loud to myself. "Please sit down and we will figure this out. Would you like a snack?"

"No, thank you. I do not eat junk food."

"There are carrots," I said hopefully.

"I had my quota for today."

I wiped the donut crumbs still on my hands with the tablecloth and was immediately embarrassed. Fortunately, she was still looking around the room.

"Annie said her teacher wanted her to take the WASL test in the Resource Room so she wouldn't distract the other, more attentive, students."

"Yes."

"And this is the Resource Room?" she asked.

"Yes."

"My Annie has difficulty being still," Mrs. Harrigan continued.

"Yes."

"She said you gave her a big ball to sit on and told her that if she needed to bounce or move, she could do so."

"Yes."

"Annie also said she felt wonderful and relaxed. She was able to finish the test without any problems, except for the writing parts. She thinks she got every answer correct, but somehow I am not as confident."

"Yes."

"She told her father and me that she wanted to go to your class every day. Some of your Resource students told her that in order to get in she had to change her last name to Oakley and learn to gallop."

“Yes.” I truly could not think of anything else to say at the moment. I was never so tongue tied, but for some reason I was not sure where this was going. Was I in trouble? Would Mrs. Schultz be storming in at any moment? Would I need to say I was leaving because the Diet Dr. Pepper was too warm in the pop machine?

She laughed. She laughed long and hard. She laughed hysterically until tears escaped from the corners of her eyes. I, too, started laughing. I looked around and found the tissue box. We both grabbed one and dabbed our eyes.

“I know this must look awfully strange, Mrs. Harrigan,” I said between breathless chuckles. “Next year, the Old Western theme will be gone and something new will take its place. Maybe we could do the final frontier – space.”

“Oh, that is wonderful. Annie will want a spacesuit and a rocket ship!”

“My sister, Maddie, is very artistically creative. She designs the themes. I give her some thoughts and ideas and she gets carried away,” I said. “In a few years, I am thinking about a time machine for the new century. It will take me that long to figure out how to convince her to do that one.”

“I think that is a great idea. At least we will have ten decades of material to work with,” Mrs. Harrigan said, and we both laughed again.

“I do not typically wear the themes on my back. That was our theatrical musical director’s horrific idea of a joke when my regular professional outfit got,” I said, then stopped mid-sentence, realizing I still had the sombrero on my head. I quickly took it off and tossed it under the table.

"Never mind, that is not what is important. So, Mrs. Harrigan, how can I help you?"

She chuckled even louder. "Please call me Margaret."

"Thank you for understanding, Margaret," I said.

"I think I can now comprehend why Annie was so excited. Can she do her schoolwork in here?" Margaret asked.

"Well, it is not as straightforward as that," I answered. "It is a complicated process."

She watched me intently and shook her head. "What do we need to do?"

"Give me a little time. I will talk to her classroom teacher first to get an idea of Annie's individual needs," I said.

"I can tell you what my husband and I believe. Annie is a bit of a conundrum. She has baffled her teachers for the last three years. Last week, I had a conference with her current fourth grade teacher. She said that Annie is a strong reader, better than most. I have always known that. She loves to read and make up stories. Her teacher also said that when it comes to math calculations, she is quite good and has an amazing memory. But now that math includes a lot of writing, Annie gets more and more distracted. She moves around a lot, drops or breaks her pencils, makes unnecessary noises, and ends up getting into trouble. The teacher says that she has been reluctant to send Annie to the office but may have to do that if she continues to refuse to work."

"Does she refuse to read?" I asked.

"Never."

"Do you or the teacher see these behaviors as being connected to writing?"

Margaret Harrigan thought awhile before answering. "I think they must be. I know this will sound strange because we truly believe Annie is very bright, but she cannot or will not write."

After taking a long breath, Mrs. Harrigan continued, "Her teacher mentioned that because Annie moves around a great deal and can't seem to sit still, that maybe there was a neurological problem. I can tell you that scared my husband and myself, so we immediately made an appointment with her pediatrician. The doctor said Annie may have ADHD. Do you know what that is?"

I wanted to laugh, but I knew she wouldn't understand why. "It stands for Attention Deficit Hyperactivity Disorder, and yes, I know what it means as well as methods that can help a child diagnosed with it."

"You mean an old cowgirl like you can treat this?" she grinned.

"Old?"

"I'm sorry. I got carried away."

"No problem, old gal." I grinned back at her.

"We asked the doctor what could be done. He said we could discuss medication. But he felt the first priority should be talking to Annie's school about testing for a learning disability."

"I agree with your doctor. Although I really haven't known Annie for very long, I suspect she may have a writing disability that is sometimes called dysgraphia."

"What is that? It sounds fatal."

"No, hardly. It basically means the inability to write."

"Oh, my goodness. Is that what she has? Can it be cured?" Mrs. Harrigan looked frightened.

"Good heavens, I am not saying that is what is going on. I will need to do some testing first to discover if she has a learning disability."

"Is that what you are doing now with this WASL testing?" she asked.

"No. The WASL is a state-required standardized test. It is used as a benchmark to discover how all fourth graders in the state of Washington compare to each other. It is also then measured with other standardized tests throughout the country. It is supposed to help determine if we as educators are up-to-speed with what children need to learn. In my opinion it is fairly ludicrous to give it to students who have had numerous assessments not only to determine eligibility for services but also to do daily progress monitoring. The WASL cannot determine if a child has a specific learning disability. Those particular assessments are given by qualified Special Education teachers like me and sometimes psychologists. They are given individually. We use those tests as a basis to determine if a child does have a specific learning disability and whether specially designed instruction is warranted."

"Do you think Annie should be tested for this?" she asked.

"What do you think? Do you want her to keep falling further behind? Do you want her to be inattentive and hide the fact that writing is difficult for her? Do you want to know why she is doing this? And more importantly, do you want her to get help?"

Margaret Harrigan looked around the staged environment that we had designed for the Resource Room at the beginning of the school year. She took a deep breath before nodding assent. "I guess I should tell you that I am good friends with the mother of one of your students. I know you can't talk about her child, and I really shouldn't be bringing it up, but I thought you might like to know."

"My lips are sealed. I can cope. Hey, if I can manage having someone's lunch deposited all over me, then I can listen to comments about my program and me."

"So that's what happened," she said.

I shook my head and gave a soft chuckle.

"My friend told me in confidence that her son was the terror of his first four years of elementary school. He was finally evaluated by you. It was determined that he had a reading disability. The parents were crushed at first, but you talked them into an IEP, they called it."

"Individualized Education Plan, yes," I replied.

"You told them that he met eligibility and qualified for something else called SDI."

"Specially designed instruction, yes," I answered again.

"He started going to your Resource Room here. My friend said it didn't happen overnight, but you taught him how to read. She said that he learned more in Reading in one year than he had in the four previous years he had been in school."

"That happens sometimes. Not always, but sometimes," I responded.

"She said her son is happier than he ever has been. He loves going to the Resource Room. She also said that he feels comfortable and isn't worried about making mistakes. She told me that her son has always been a bit cocky, but his self-esteem has skyrocketed."

"I'm liking the idea of the space theme for next year," I said.

"So, what happens next?"

"First, I will talk to Annie's teacher. Next, I will bring up what we talked about at our next Guidance team meeting. This team is a mixture of teachers, administrators, specialists, and Special Education staff with the purpose of discussing any child in the school who might have concerns that need to be addressed. Then before we decide if an evaluation is warranted, we will meet with you and your husband. Your signed permission is required before we can begin."

"Then she will be able to start in the Resource Room?"

"Not quite. First, we will go over the test results with you. If she qualifies, we will design that individualized education plan I mentioned earlier. I know it sounds complicated, but it will all make sense eventually."

"How did you get into this line of work, if you don't mind my asking?"

"I don't mind at all. I love to talk about it. But it is a very long story and I think it is starting to get dark outside," I said, looking out the window and watching the rain.

"Another time then. Please let us take you to some country western tavern and have a good chat," she suggested.

"I would love that, but I'm afraid even though I might fit in, you definitely would not!"

We both laughed as she got up and retrieved her purse. "It sounds like we will be ready to board an Old West stagecoach."

"At least you know you won't have to get a horse."

"Thank you," she said, "in more ways than one."

"You're welcome."

"By the way," she said before she walked out the door, "how did you manage the authentic Old West smells?"

"Just lucky, I guess."

Mrs. Harrigan turned and left. I reached around and grabbed the last of the glazed donuts. My nose twitched at the sweet smells of the icing masking the other scents as I moved it instinctively to my mouth.

Mrs. Harrigan returned, hanging onto the doorway frame. "One more thing."

I tossed the donut behind my back and dropped it on the table with the previous one. "Yes?" I asked.

"I think you could truly help Annie," she said.

"I will try."

Margaret Harrigan nodded and walked away. I surveyed the room once more with a grin. I finally found some sponges and paper towels and quickly cleaned up the debris lingering on the tables, chairs, and desks. I threw away the food that could not be used the next day. The wrapped healthy bars that no one ate could remain. I looked longingly at the remaining bear claw. It seemed to be calling me. Smiling, I picked it up and tossed the sweet temptation into the garbage can. Next, I grabbed my purse from the desk drawer and my rain jacket from the coatrack. After I walked to the door, I stood motionless by the light switch before turning it off. Instead, I walked back over to the snack table. Returning to the door, I shut off the lights, closed the door, and smiled as I chomped on two carrots. "Oh, well, I haven't had my quota today yet," my words echoed out loud to an eerily deserted school hallway.

CHAPTER 21

The Reader

"Mrs. Wright, Mrs. Wright!"

I squinted toward the screeching at the end of the darkened hallway. "Hello?" I questioned the shadow racing closer to me.

"Do not descend into darkness on me, Mrs. Wright. Turn on the light!"

That could only be Tommy. I knew that before he skidded to a stop. He always produced the cleverest statements. Without embarrassment I often loved repeating them as my own when chatting with other teachers.

"What are you doing here, Tommy?" I asked, turning the lights on again, shrugging off my jacket and putting down my purse. "School has been out for a couple of hours now."

"I know. Significant grasp of the obvious, Mrs. Wright," he said with a smirk.

"And?" I asked stifling a groan.

"My mom made me come with her to some dreary parent meeting in the library. It has something to do with volunteering at the upcoming Science Fair. She said I could not stay home with Dad because we would get into all sorts of mischief."

"I understand, but why are you back in the Resource Room rather than staying in the library?" I asked.

"Well, it is very easy to comprehend if you think about it," he said, looking at the now covered snack table.

"You want a snack?" I asked.

"No, it smells in here."

"Yes" was all I could say.

Tommy continued his explanation as he walked toward my free-time area in the corner of the classroom. "Mom told me to grab a book and read quietly in the back of the room. I only asked if she was trying to mess with my mind. It may have come out a little loud because every one of those women turned their heads and gave me the 'mom' look."

"And?"

"I snuck out when they turned back to their dull conversations, and I headed here. I thought maybe there would be a baby book I could try to figure out in the OK Corral Book Barn," he said.

"Not a bad idea. There are plenty of books you can read here. And, I might add, in the library, too," I said to him.

"You have got to be kidding. You can be amusing sometimes, Mrs. Wright, but you are going overboard now. Everyone in this school knows that I can't read!"

"Maybe everyone is stuck in your head, and it is only you who thinks that."

Tommy looked at me as if I were demented. "OK, now you are sounding a bit like me. This is getting frightening."

"Come here," I said to Tommy, motioning him to follow me to the table in the front of the classroom where the tests were gathered. I found his and opened it to the first page. I covered everything except the directions at the top.

"What are you doing?" he asked.

"What does this say?"

He looked at me and back at the writing on the page. "Use only a number two pencil. Mechanical pencils or pens are not allowed."

"I thought you said you couldn't read," I said, smiling. "I think you are smarter than the average bear."

"I don't know where you come up with these weird expressions, but in here it should be horse, not bear."

"Well, I think you are pretty smart after all," I added.

"No, I'm not. That was easy because you repeated it a million times today!"

"So, you can read it now. That is what reading is. You do it over and over again and presto magic, you have it memorized. Of course, it takes time and practice, but before you know it, you are reading."

Neither of us spoke for a few minutes. Tommy went back over to the book barn area and picked up a book after rummaging through a few. "Some of these are out of order. I put them back in the right places. This would really drive Shane crazy. He is the best reader in the world, but he can't stand it when something is not in order."

"Did you find something that interests you?"

"I think so. I will convince Mom to read it to me tonight a thousand times, then I will read it back to her."

"Sounds like a good plan," I said.

"Or payback," he said with a wicked grin.

I only smiled while attempting to clean up a few things on the snack table.

"Will the testing be easier tomorrow?" Tommy asked, acting uncharacteristically shy.

"I don't know. My mother used to say, 'If there is one thing you know, it's that you never know.'"

"Do you get your smarts from your mom?"

"I hope so."

"You never know," Tommy said looking at me with a mischievous frown. "My mom says I get mine from my dad. She calls him Alec, but his real name is George."

"I think I hear your mom yelling your name all the way from the library," I said, lifting my head up and turning toward the door.

"That meeting must be over, or they ended it before everyone died of boredom."

"Time to go home, Tommy," I said.

"You, too, Mrs. Wright," Tommy said, looking at me with his head askew. "Do you think you could wear something a little less weird tomorrow?"

"Like maybe a saloon girl ensemble," a breathless voice said as Tommy's mother appeared around the corner and peeked into the room. She looked directly at Tom and made a sound of extreme annoyance.

"Hi, Mom. What brings you down here? Do you want to learn how to read, too?"

"Sorry, Mrs. Smart," I addressed his mother. "Tommy was just picking out a book to take home and read."

"He had a whole library of books."

"Mrs. Wright helped me find a great one and had a wonderful suggestion how you can help me tonight," he added.

"Oh, does she now?" Tom's mom said to him but looked directly at me.

At that awkward moment, the tension was suddenly broken when Mrs. Harrigan rushed back into the room. "Oh, I do apologize for interrupting. I forgot my hat and coat." She grabbed her items quickly and turned to leave.

"No problem at all," Mrs. Smart said quickly. "We were just leaving. By the way, I must say that I absolutely love your hat. Where did you get it?"

Mrs. Harrigan turned back around. "Why thank you. Most people don't even notice. I made it."

"Really? You are so clever."

"Please let me introduce you," I managed to cut in. "Mrs. Margaret Harrigan, this is Mrs. Elsie Smart, Tommy's mother."

"Harrigan?" Tommy queried. "As in Annie Harrigan?"

"Yes, she is my daughter."

"Annie is so super cool. I suggested she change her name to Oakley and get a horse. It seemed more fitting for this year's round-up. She loved the idea."

"Sorry." Mrs. Smart looked at Annie's mother and shrugged.

Mrs. Harrigan's slight smile turned into a huge laugh. She turned to me and added as if making a joke, "I dread to imagine what next year's theme will be. Can I call your sister and give her my suggestions?"

"I have a few ideas of my own," Mrs. Smart added.

"Now *I* dread to think," I responded to both women.

Now everyone was hysterical. Through her laughter, Mrs. Smart said, "I suggested she wear a saloon girl costume tomorrow."

"I was thinking a sheriff without a gun." Mrs. Harrigan laughed again.

"Hey, Mrs. Wright, next year you should do *Wizard of Oz*, then we can call you a munchkin," Tommy said. "And you could bring in a winged monkey."

My tenuous glee faded. "Good heavens, I hope not," I said.

"So, Margaret Harrigan, how are you with Science Fairs?" Elsie Smart asked, still chuckling.

"I don't really know."

"That's one thing you always know," Tommy said to everyone.

Both women looked at him oddly but continued their discussion. "I was just roped into being in charge of the Science Fair," Elsie said to Margaret.

"Roped?" Mrs. Harrigan asked. And they both laughed again.

"What do you do for a living, if I may ask?"

"I am a lawyer, and my husband is the superintendent at another school district," Mrs. Harrigan answered. "And you?"

"My husband and I own and operate a bagel deli in the city."

"It sounds like this Science Fair exhibition is right up our alley," Mrs. Harrigan said, shaking her head and pretending to be pretentious. "So, what are your qualifications for this elite Science Fair position?"

"Oh, believe me, please feel free to step into my shoes."

"If the Science Fair organization team is next year, those shoes could be my thematic ruby red slippers," I said adding to the merriment at my own expense.

Their new camaraderie continued as they waved goodbye to me and wandered down the hallway chatting amicably. Tommy followed closely behind as I gazed from the doorway wondering how I would ever figure out a way to talk my sister out of a *Wizard of Oz* theme for next year.

"Hey, Mrs. Wright!" Tommy turned around to face me but was managing to walk backwards at the same time. "You are pretty clever, after all!"

He turned back around. His galloping footsteps faded into silence while his words echoed in my mind. Eventually, the stillness surrounded me. After a full day of steady rain beating a melodic background noise, it had ended. "I don't think I will take the umbrella," I thought to myself, but grabbed it anyway. I pulled on my rain jacket, lifted the hood over my head, and picked up my purse before shutting off the lights once more, exiting the classroom and closing the door. In a seemingly obsessive manner, I ceremoniously touched the sign on the wall and felt a sense of joy surge through my soul – The Resource Room, Mrs. Wright, Teacher.

ACKNOWLEDGEMENTS

Over the years, there are numerous people who shape our lives. When thinking about who to directly acknowledge for helping me with this particular book, I must look back into my own history with a fondness for a time gone by and those I'll never forget. They made it possible and will probably never know the impact they have had.

Also, I am not sure I ever gave my sister, Judith Dickenson Ackaret, the recognition she deserves for her incredible creative talent. Without her help, I doubt those classroom environment themes would have existed. They set the standard and the unique positive feel for a successful Resource Room over the years. I also wish to thank her for encouraging my writing and her advice, regardless if I took it or not. And to her husband, Jerry Ackaret, for publishing this book and *Uniquely Stella*, my first novel, through JAT Trax Studios. Judith and Jerry are currently designing and will implement the upcoming Podcast *Resource Remedies* that I will be hosting.

How did I get so lucky to have Nancy Emrick as my incredible lifelong friend? She read the first draft and gave me the inspiration I truly wanted and needed. My appreciation also goes out to Nancy & Barry Meyer, Mimi Menenberg, and Pam Lee who graciously acted as beta readers to give me insightful comments on my manuscript. And to Gin Duchman who read the very first and very rough draft and told me that it is the way it was and had to be told! It was fun to model a supporting character with her in mind. I know I made Mrs. Duchamp into a saint, but that is how I remember the many incredible staff assistants who I worked with over the years. I took the best of all of them. I also worked with more school staff than I can name during my 36-year career. I will be forever grateful for all the hard work and how they enriched my life and that of our students.

I would like to give a special shout out to Sue Campbell and the staff at Pages & Platforms. Bits and pieces of this manuscript had been on the floor, in boxes, and on the shelf for years. Sue helped me set my mind in gear, stop procrastinating and finally finish what I wanted to do for so long.

Thank you as well to Linda Franklin for being such an incredible editor!

To my wonderful husband, Russell. I'm still not sure how he puts up with me when I agonize over this, that, or the other thing. But he stays upbeat, reads everything, and encourages the best from me. I am so lucky to have found him.

Amy, my daughter, must get a special mention. She knew instinctively when to give me space. There are quotes from her in this book. She was once a Resource student. I wish she had been in my room. And to my surrogate daughter, Shelby Kinney, for helping with marketing and social media.

Finally, and probably most importantly, are my students. Many years ago, when I was quite young and still a novice, I asked my students if they would remember me when I was 70 years old. One little boy said, "How could I ever forget you. You are stuck in my head for all eternity!" I don't know where he is now, but I wish he knew that one of the characters in *Uniquely Us – Tales from a Resource Room* is exactly him. To all my former students, you will stay in my head for all eternity.

ABOUT THE AUTHOR

Deborah M. Menenberg received a Bachelor of Science degree in Psychology, Speech Communication and Theatre Arts from Southern Oregon College. After obtaining a master's degree in Special Education at the University of Oregon, she started what would become a thirty-six-year career as a Special Education Resource Room teacher, for which she is listed in *Who's Who in American Teachers*. Deborah has always been a storyteller. She would often tell her students stories, encouraging them to write their own creative adventures and occasionally act them out. Many of her own classroom tales would be told in letters or emails to friends and family. She also wrote and directed many school plays and taught numerous drama classes. Apart from teaching, Deborah toured the inland waterways of Great Britain on a narrowboat performing with the Daystar Theatre Company. When home in Oregon or Washington, she directed or acted in various community theatre productions. Currently, Deborah is retired and lives on a floating home in Portland, Oregon, with her husband, Russell, and their Golden Retriever, Flyer.

ALSO BY DEBORAH M. MENENBERG:

Uniquely Stella (a Historical Fiction novel)

At the end of World War II, 19-year-old Stella leaves her job at a war factory in Chicago to embark on a journey of unexpected consequences. Boarding a train headed west, she meets her new best friend, a young black woman. Together they learn the complexities and depth of discrimination and prejudice. These lessons fuel Stella's poignant and powerful journey that truly begins with the birth of her Down's syndrome daughter.

When eventually confronting a school system that can legally refuse to educate those that don't fit in, Stella becomes intent on giving voice to an ignored population. Inspired by a true story, *Uniquely Stella* combines love, humor, and grace into a tale reminding us that the policies and laws governing us should always be guided by a passion for equality.

Praise for *Uniquely Stella*

- WINNER of Red City Book Review – Fan Favorite category
- "The heart of this novel pumps fiercely, and Stella's resolute optimism is a poultice for today's troubled times." – Red City Book Review
- "This book is such an inspiring portrait of human kindness." – Goodreads review
- "A glorious dream to read." – Guest review

MAKING CONNECTIONS: www.deborahmenenberg.com